Red the Were Hunter

Fairelle Book One

By Rebekah R. Ganiere

ISBN: 978-1-63300-001
ISBN: 978-1-63300-001-8
Cover art by Rebekah R. Ganiere

Fallen Angel Press
1040 N. Las Palmas Blvd.
Bldg. 24 Suite 203
Los Angeles, CA 90038
www.FallenAngelPress.com

Ordering Information:
Orders by U.S. trade bookstores and wholesalers. Please visit
www.FallenAngelPress.com.
Printed in the United States of America

DEDICATION

For Bug, who's always believed in me.

Pereum, Fairelle Year 200
PROLOGUE

In the year 200, in the city of Pereum, the heart of Fairelle, King Isodor lay on his deathbed. With all of Fairelle united under his banner, his four rival sons vied for the crown. One-by-one, the brothers called forth a djinn named Xereus from Shaidan, the daemon realm, to grant a single wish. But Xereus tricked the brothers, twisting their wishes.

The eldest wished to forever be bloodthirsty in battle, and was thus transformed into a Vampire. The second wished for the unending loyalty of his men, and was turned into a Werewolf. The third asked for the ability to manipulate the elements of Fairelle; he became physically weak, but mighty in magick, a Fae. And the last asked to rule the sea. A Nereid.

When the king died, each brother took a piece of Fairelle for himself and waged war for control of the rest. Xereus, having been called forth so many times, tore a rift between his daemonic plane and Fairelle, allowing thousands of daemons to pour into Pereum.

Years upon years of bloody warring went by, all races fighting for control, and eventually the daemons gained dominion of the heart of Fairelle. Realizing that all lands would soon fall into the daemons' control, the High Elders of the Fae and the Mages from the south combined their magicks to seal the rift. The daemons were banished back to their own plane, but Pereum was wiped off the map in the process, leaving only charred waste behind, forever, known as The Daemon Wastelands.

Upon the day of the rift closing, a Mage soothsayer prophesied of the healing of Fairelle. Over the next thousand years, the races continued to war against each other, waiting for the day when the ancient prophesies would begin.

Nine prophesies, a thousand years old, to unite the lands and heal Fairelle. The first is the prophecy of the wolves.

Volkzene, Fairelle 1200 years A.D. (After Daemons)

CHAPTER ONE

Another girl had been taken. One moment the small village of Volkzene was silent, with Redlynn drifting off to sleep to the rhythmical sounds of her clock ticking; the next a scream pierced the night.

Redlynn leapt from her bed, grabbed her sword, and tore out to the street. People in their nightclothes, brandishing torches and lanterns, filled the village center.

"Where are they?" she called at the nearest neighbor.

"Cantrel's." The woman ran for the safety of her home.

Anya! Redlynn sprinted toward the south edge of the village. Her best friend was on guard alone at the Cantrel's hut. Breathing hard, the cold night wind whipped her wavy, red hair into her face and raised goose bumps on her skin. The sound of her blood pumping in her ears drowned out the buzz of the village folk.

"Anya," she screamed. "Anya, where are you?"

Redlynn charged through the crowd gathered outside the hut. "Move," she yelled. The other members of the Sisterhood and villagers backed away at the sight of her.

The smell of blood hit her. She stepped over the threshold, the horror slapping her with force. Her heart faltered and a cry escaped her lips.

"No-o-o-o!" she screamed. "Anya!"

Anya's mangled body lay sprawled on the floor, her bow still clutched in her fingers. Redlynn's mind numbed, unable to process the scene. She spun slowly on the spot. An arrow stuck in the wall next to the door. Bits of wood were strewn about from the smashed kitchen table. Coals tumbled from the fire, and little more than charred cinders remained of the curtains. A pail of water lay discarded nearby. The Cantrels huddled on their bed in the adjoining room, Mrs. Cantrel sobbed into her husband's chest.

"Sasha, my Sasha," Mrs. Cantrel moaned.

Anger and despair ripped through Redlynn's gut. Her sword hit the floor with a clatter and she collapsed to her knees, gathering her best friend's bloody body in her arms. She sucked in large gasps of air, tears streaming down her cheeks. *The very last of my loved ones.*

Anya stared blankly into the night, her eyes transfixed and cloudy. Redlynn stroked her hair and tried in vain to piece the skin together on Anya's neck and torso. At just nineteen, Anya had been through so much in her short life. Too much, and now it was over. Sadness gave way to anger, and bile scorched her throat.

"This is your fault," Mrs. Cantrel screeched, pointing at Redlynn. "Where were you? You were supposed to stand guard with Anya."

Redlynn swallowed the angry words she wanted to say. "I'll find Sasha," she promised the teary-eyed mother.

"Find her? Those beasts have probably already torn her to bits. You're the protector, and where were you? Asleep. To let my Sasha be taken, and poor Anya to be murdered. If you can't even do the one thing we've kept you around for, what good are you?"

The words slapped Redlynn in the face. Her throat went dry. She searched for something to say. Something to soothe the mother, to soothe herself. "I'll find her."

"Get out of my house, Cursed!" Mrs. Cantrel screamed.

Redlynn's heart thundered in her chest. She laid Anya down, grabbed her sword, and pushed out the door, past the crowd of Sisters and villagers. Running flat out, she made for the village gate.

"Red!"

The sound of her name stopped her. Breathing hard, her body surged with adrenaline. Her head pounded with the need for vengeance. Her heart ached from the pain of Mrs. Cantrel's words.

"I hope you aren't thinking of doing anything foolish." Lillith stepped calmly from the shadows, her red stone necklace glowing faintly in the dim light.

Redlynn locked eyes on the head of her Order and ground her teeth.

"You know it's forbidden to go into the woods."

"We need to go out there. Strike them now. Take the fight to them and end this." Redlynn continued toward the gate. "We need to become the hunters we used to be. Not the village guard we are now."

Members of the Sisterhood gathered around.

"Do not defy me on this, Red." Lillith crossed her arms over her chest. "It won't end well for you if you do."

Redlynn closed her eyes and sucked in the chilled night air, trying to get her mind to focus. Anya was dead. Another girl was gone, and they just stood around arguing, like always.

Sasha made the second girl this month; twelve all together. There had been five new girls inducted as full-fledged members of the Sisterhood this year. All of them carried off by Weres. It made no sense. The Weres hadn't attacked the village since before her time. What changed?

A frigid wind hit her skin. Frost from the ground seeped through her stockings, making her shiver in her nightgown. The rage inside dimmed, giving way for a need to understand what had happened.

5

"Tell me," she demanded, wiping tears from her cheeks. "What happened this time?"

Lillith's voice carried into the night for all to hear. "The Weres came in a pack of three. Snuck in and stole Sasha out of her bed, like all the others."

Redlynn let out a shuddered breath. Anya, a good fighter, would've been no match for three. No one was, but perhaps Redlynn herself. *I shouldn't have left her alone.*

"Who was on watch?" she asked.

The Sisters looked at each other.

"Who saw them come through the gate?" Her eyes raked over the group of women.

"I did." Lillith's back straightened.

"Why was the alarm not sounded?" she yelled, taking a step closer. "How could you let this happen?"

Lillith's gaze flicked to the crowd, then snapped to Redlynn. "Don't take that tone of voice with me, Red. I am the Head of the Order, not you."

Redlynn gripped her sword tightly, trying to hold her temper in check.

"We need to take care of Anya," one of the Sisters said. "Before the moon passes."

Redlynn took a deep, cleansing breath. She had to keep it together. "I'll do it."

Lillith stepped in Redlynn's path, blocking her. "You don't need to–"

"I will do it." She glared at Lillith before stepping around her.

Lillith glanced away, as everyone did from her cursed golden eyes. "We'll move her to the Hall and prepare, while you clean up."

It was not a request.

The rest of the Sisterhood watched the exchange. Redlynn ground her teeth together so hard her jaw ached. For years they'd

6

been waiting for the day when she'd challenge Lillith for control as Head of the Order. Swallowing her anger and pride, she turned from them and headed home.

She dragged her sword, heavy as an ox's yoke, through the mud to the other end of the village. Her feet were past being numb in the bitter November cold. Fiery pins and needles pricked at her soles with every sloppy step she took.

I deserved this pain. It should have been me. If it had been, Sasha would still be here, Anya would be alive, and we'd have three less Weres in the woods to worry about. The pain in her body and the pain in her soul were the price she paid for allowing Anya to stand guard alone tonight. *I shouldn't have given in. I should have stayed with her.*

The wary glances from the villagers made loneliness swell within her. Out of reflex, she grasped the small oval locket hanging loosely beneath her nightgown, and thought of her mother.

She let her feet carry her down the street, past the deserted training ground. Wind whistled through the archery targets and sparring dummies. Moist air from the small fountain in front of the village hall made Redlynn's gown cling to her legs. She glanced sideways at the village council, who gathered in the doorway of the building that served as school, church and meeting house. They watched her go.

Why did she stay? She asked herself for the millionth time. Why couldn't she just find a new place? A better place? She knew the answer all too well. She'd promised her mother. Redlynn hiccuped a sob and turned from the council's gaze, unwilling to let them witness her shame.

Reaching her wood-and-thatched home, the sounds of the village chatter died away. She walked in the still-open door.

"Dammit!" The fire had gone out. She hurled her sword across the front room, leaving it stuck into the wall of her bedroom. She slammed the front door behind her.

Snatching up the fire poker, she stabbed at the crumbling log; sparks swirled up into the flue. Redlynn ignored her quivering chin and concentrated all her efforts into teasing the fire alight. Tears threatened to spill, but she refused to free them. She wouldn't show more weakness. She would swallow it down until the right time, and then she'd get revenge.

The fire caught. Redlynn threw down the poker and grabbed her red cloak from the hook, wrapping it over her shoulders. With trembling fingers, she stripped off her muddy stockings, tossing them into the water basin to soak. Anya's blood caked Redlynn's hands and gown.

Redlynn tied her long, red hair up in a leather strap, pushed the sticky nightgown down her body to the floor, and plunged her hands into the water bucket. She scrubbed her flesh from under her cloak, with her bloodied gown. She couldn't scrub hard enough; the metallic scent of iron filled her senses.

Biting her cheek, she tried to stop the nausea from taking over. Blood never affected her in battle; when every piece of her was fighting for her life, nothing else mattered. But given more mundane circumstances, the scent and the texture of it, the fact that it was Anya's, caused her to almost faint. She grabbed the table where the wash basin sat, trying to keep herself steady. When the darkness receded from her vision, she threw the gown into the basin.

Shivering, she hurried to her bedroom. She dropped her cloak and pulled on a clean tunic. Looking down, she spotted another of her flaws. A purple birthmark, shaped like a wolf, above her left breast. Tonight the heavy burdens of her life seemed to be piling on top of her.

Redlynn shoved her legs into her breeches and noticed her mother's bow leaning against the wall.

How many Weres had her mother and grandmother taken down with that bow? Her lineage went all the way back to the first

Sister herself. Were hunting was in her blood. Not this pitiful existence she now lived. Her Sisterhood sword, with the wolf's head handle and ruby eyes, hung still lodged in the wall. She stared at the sword, and heat rushed into her chest. She knew what she must do.

She had to kill the beast responsible for ordering the kidnapping of the girls, and the death of Anya. She needed to drench her sword in the blood of the Were King. To feel the sweet satisfaction of vengeance as she ran him through.

Redlynn grabbed the bow, quiver, cloak and her bag. Filling the bag to the brim with herbs, clothes, food and everything else she might need for her trek, she looked around the home that she and her mother had built with their bare hands. All the pieces of her mother's life hung around her. She clutched her locket again as her heart squeezed, remembering the past.

The buckskin satchel her mother had used for her midwife visits. Her mother's tea cup set, adorned with giant yellow sungold flowers, passed down for generations. The wicker rocking chair that her mother had sat in to sing, knit, and tell stories to Redlynn.

Come on. Be optimistic. You might not die. Redlynn snorted and reminded herself that she wasn't the optimistic type.

When the Head of the Order had first founded the village decades ago, there'd been over sixty members of the Sisterhood. The Sisters used to hunt the Weres nightly. Now only a handful of active-duty Sisters spent their time as the village guard, trying to fend off the attacks. It had to end. She wouldn't waste away in this hellhole any longer. Redlynn strode to the wall in her bedroom, yanked down her sword, and set it with her pack.

Her mind was made up. She'd had enough. Her promise to her mother that she'd protect the village wasn't being fulfilled by sitting on her rear, waiting for the Weres to attack. She was sick of girls being taken, never to be heard from again. But Redlynn knew better than to try and fool herself. She wasn't doing this for the villagers; she was doing this for Anya, for her mother. For herself.

Just a few more hours and she'd shed the last of her tears while she cleansed Anya, lock away her sadness deep inside, and allow the anger to take over. Tomorrow she'd become like the Sisters of old. No longer would she wait around for the Weres to attack. She'd raid their caves and drive them out. She'd become Red, The Werewolf Hunter.

"Hey Red," said Yanti, in her cheerful ten-year-old voice. "I came to see if you were okay."

Redlynn pushed past her, closed the front door, and stepped down onto the frosty dirt road. "Yanti, I don't have time today. I'm sorry."

"Oh."

The sound of Yanti's defeated voice made Redlynn stop in her tracks.

"I brought you this." Yanti held out a small basket. "I figured you wouldn't have time for breakfast."

Way to go, Redlynn. Make the kiddies cry. Redlynn laid her hand on Yanti's shoulder. Yanti continued to look at the basket. She used her fist to lift the girl's chin and gave Yanti a small smile. "Thank you. If you leave it on my table, I'll eat it when I'm done."

"Okay." Yanti pushed her hair behind her ear.

"Then you run off to school and training. I don't want you wandering about today. Today is a weeping day."

"I'll head straight there, Red, I promise." Yanti smiled again. "I want to be the Head of the Order someday and wear the red stone necklace, like Lillith's." Yanti scrunched up her face. "Red, why aren't you the Head of the Sisterhood, like your grandmother?"

Redlynn's eye twitched. "There's more to being the Head of the Sisterhood than just wearing pretty things and living in a nice home, you know."

"I know, but the necklace is so shiny. And she has a matching mirror, have you seen it?"

A chill raced up Redlynn's spine. "Where did *you* see it?"

"She was sick a few months back, and my mother had me take her some broth. It was sitting on her nightstand. It must be pretty important to her, because when I tried to touch it, she yelled at me and told me to get out. Said it was a present from a special admirer, and no one could touch it but her."

Redlynn swallowed hard. "Off to school."

Yanti smiled and headed into Redlynn's house, then ran back out. "Bye, Red!" she called. "I'm gonna be just like you someday!"

Redlynn shivered. Yanti deserved to be a mother, married to a wealthy farmer, passing on her golden curls and green eyes to a brood of chubby children, far from the death and despair of Volkzene. And if Yanti and Redlynn were lucky, she'd be able to do just that. All she needed was for Redlynn to succeed in killing the Were King. Redlynn's chest tightened as Mrs. Cantrel's words from the night before hit her again.

And then, maybe if she succeeded, the villagers would stop using her for protection only, and finally accept her as one of their own, despite her strange eyes.

CHAPTER TWO

Redlynn tread wearily to the town hall. The wind still whistled through the main muddy road of the village. She pulled her cloak close and passed the Borwen's pig pen. The village felt quiet and lonely at the early hour. A Sister exited her house, stopped short when she saw Redlynn, gave a weak smile, and then hurried toward the village hall. Redlynn sniffed, but said nothing. She was used to it. The village wanted her there, only because of who her ancestors were, and her expertise with a bow and sword.

A thatcher loaded up his wagon, not sparing her a moment's glance. A group of young farmers stomped silently through the muddy streets toward their plots of land, south of the village wall.

At the village center, Redlynn pushed open the large doors to the Sisterhood headquarters. The scent of candle wax and incense wafted out. Anya's body lay on the altar, atop a white linen sheet. Tall beeswax candles lined the walls, and robed sisters crushed Volkzene flowers into a paste. She approached Anya without a word, her stomach roiling with acid. Everyone stopped moving. She unfastened her cloak and set it on a wooden bench.

Redlynn's mind flooded with the memory of Anya's last words, and she swallowed hard.

"I can do this, Red. Trust me."

Lillith moved forward in her cream ceremonial garb, the Sisterhood Bible in her hands. Three more Sisters joined her and began the Song of Lament to accompany Lillith's sacred prayer. Redlynn let the words drift away, concentrating only on the task at hand. Picking up the bone needle and white thread, she began at Anya's throat. She blinked rapidly, trying to stop her tears. She couldn't mess this up. Anya deserved the best.

With each piercing of the skin, Redlynn begged for Anya's forgiveness. For each tug of the thread, she swore to avenge her friend's death. She memorized every detail of Anya's wounds. Every bite, every tear. Counting them, till they all blended together in the blur of her tears.

When she finished, Redlynn took the Volkzene paste and pressed the crushed flowers into Anya's wounds, remembering each laugh, each smile, each moment of friendship they'd shared. The way Anya used to push her hair behind her ear. The determination in her eyes as she aimed her bow. The nights of holding Redlynn as she'd sobbed over the death of her mother.

The drone of Lillith's voice stopped after what seemed like an eternity. Redlynn reached down, kissed Anya one last time.

"Sleep well, my sister. May you find peace on your new journey. My sword will bring thee vengeance, and my heart hold thee always."

Redlynn didn't even see the cloth that she wrapped Anya in through her stream of tears.

Redlynn couldn't cope with the burning of her best friend's body. To smell the flesh and hair as it charred. So instead, with eyes drained of water, like the Daemon Wastelands, she went home and collected her things. Her heart heavy, she looked at her mother's portrait. Redlynn wondered once more why she resembled neither of her parents.

Keeping to the shadows of her neighboring houses, she reached the dirt road and crossed through the wooden perimeter fencing. No one stood guard, again. So few Sisters remained in the village. Redlynn remembered a time when the Sisters lived to be eighty or longer. Now few of the Sisters lived beyond fifty, if they survived childbirth. For a moment she wondered if she was doing the right thing. But she reminded herself that if she succeeded, they'd be safe indefinitely.

She turned, heading across the green toward the woods. Drawing near the tree line, she heard someone rushing up behind her.

"Red!"

She'd kept moving, ignoring Lillith's call.

"Redlynn! As Head of the Order, I command you to stop now!"

Redlynn halted and turned. Lillith's ample chest heaved up and down.

"Where do you think you are going?" Lillith tried to catch her breath.

"Where does it look like?"

"I have forbidden anyone from entering the forest. My rules are law here."

She said nothing. Redlynn wasn't known for living by Lillith's many rules. Unlike the other villagers, Redlynn wasn't afraid of Lillith. With Anya gone now, she had nothing to lose.

"We need you here for protection," Lillith continued.

"You can do it."

"Me? I'm the Head of the Order; who'd lead us if I die?"

Redlynn's head snapped up and she met Lillith's stare. The other woman glanced away. Her mother should've been the Head of the Sisterhood, like her ancestors before her. But due to Lillith's scheming, her mother had been discredited. She didn't know all the details. The denouncement had been held in a secret Sisterhood meeting, before Redlynn had become a member. But she'd seen firsthand how it'd crushed and ultimately killed her mother.

"Then I guess you better start training the men to protect their daughters," Redlynn bit out.

"Surely you jest? It's been the Sisterhood. Always the Sisterhood. For as long as there have been Weres, there have been Sisters. They go hand in hand, they—" Lillith stopped short.

Redlynn studied Lillith's face, and Lillith glanced away again. That nagging feeling that Lillith was keeping something from the Sisterhood stirred within Redlynn once more.

Pulling herself to her full height, Lillith tilted her chin up and glared at Redlynn. "If you leave now, you'll be cast out."

Redlynn smiled slightly. There it was. The final ultimatum. She wondered how long Lillith had dreamed of this moment. The threat meant nothing to Redlynn though. If she killed the King of the Weres, she'd be able to finally leave Volkzene and make a new life for herself. And if she didn't...

"I can live with that." Redlynn walked into the forest.

Lillith huffed behind her. "I mean it, Red! If you go, don't come back."

"Maybe you can find out how the Weres got into the village without the alarm going off while I'm gone," she yelled over her shoulder.

*****

Lillith ran into her moderate stone home and closed the door, locking it behind herself. She threw her hands over her face and screamed. What was she going to do? Red had defied her and gone into the woods. Her job was to keep the Sisters away from the wolves, and she'd failed.

She looked around at her fine things. Her beautiful furniture, her fine linens, her china. All things afforded her because of her position. They'd quickly be ripped away if she didn't keep her part of the bargain. The people she answered to were not ones to be trifled with.

They'd shown her the way to seize control of the Sisterhood, but it was with the promise that she'd keep the Sisters contained. And she had, with one exception.

15

Lillith forced herself to focus and weigh her options. She could tell Dragos, and suffer the punishment. She could follow Red and kill her. Or she could wait and see. The first option was sure to be a death sentence, and the second might be, as well.

She blew out a heavy breath. She'd just have to wait. It was possible that Red would find nothing, or that she'd be killed by the wolves. Possibly something worse. Lillith's eyes narrowed. Something worse…

She smiled to herself and walked quickly into her bedroom. An ornate mirror sat on her dressing table. She settled into a chair in front of the mirror and pressed the inlaid red stone. It glowed brightly. The surface of the mirror shimmered.

"Terona, of Tanah Darah," she commanded.

*****

Wolvenglen Forest warmed in the early spring light. A layer of dew laded the thick brush. The scent of moist dirt and leaves soothed Redlynn as always. She hadn't realized how much she'd missed running through the trees till that moment. In her loneliness they comforted her like old friends. She'd been forbidden from coming into the woods since Lillith had taken over as Head of the Order.

Redlynn's chest tightened and she clutched her locket, as she adjusted to the flood of childhood memories: her mother, laughing and singing while picking herbs, teaching her which berries to pick, or how to take leaves without damaging the plants, lying on a bed of moss as sunlight warmed her skin, the taste of cool river water, a glimpse of her mother hugging someone.

Redlynn hopped over a rock, heading toward the northwest area of Wolvenglen Forest. Once as a girl she'd tracked a group of Weres, led by a giant red one. She'd been hunting while her mother gathered herbs, and she'd spotted them near the caves. She was counting on them still subsisting there.

Redlynn trudged through ancient redwoods, stopping an hour later to fill her satchel with mushrooms and berries. She sucked the juice out of the sweet, purple draepons. The sun trickling down through the dense foliage, lighting on delicate violets sprouting from the ground. A blue-green hummingbird darted back and forth before continuing on.

A doe with her baby froze yards from where Redlynn sat. The doe's ears swiveled and her tail flicked, sensing danger. After a last hesitation, the doe fled from her presence.

"They don't like me, Mama." She'd been gathering herbs one morning, when she was six.

"Not true, Red. They fear the queen of the forest, as all animals should," her mother replied.

There was a snap behind her. Stiffening, Redlynn removed her bow from her back in a fluid movement and notched an arrow. Her bowstring groaned from being pulled taut.

Another twig snapped and she trained her sight ten degrees to the right. The leaves rustled on a plumor bush. Her bicep quaked with the strain of steadying her string. Breathing slow and deep, she held still, waiting for the attack. Adrenaline coursed through her body.

Closer... closer... *wait for it... wait...* A warthog thundered through the brush and charged. She loosed the arrow and it flew true, hitting the beast in the eye. The animal squealed and crashed to a halt, mere feet from where she stood.

Redlynn blew out a ragged breath, her blood thumping in her ears. A warthog. Not even close to a Were. If she were nearer to home, she'd drag it to the village and have food enough for months. As it was, she'd have to leave it. *What a waste.* She set her foot on the animal's shoulder for leverage and yanked the arrow free. Wiping the blood on her boot, she stuck the arrow into her quiver.

At nightfall Redlynn searched for a secure place to sleep. A tree with a hollow trunk and a slightly clear area around it caught her eye. She made her way over and peered inside. If she curled up some, it'd be large enough. Redlynn shook off her gear and pushed it through the hole, then unstrapped her bedroll and shoved it in, as well.

After setting up her things, she used a rock to dig in the damp earth, shaping a fire pit and surrounding it with stones. Normally she wouldn't try to attract attention by building such a large fire, but if it were large enough, maybe she could draw the Weres out.

Laying the base with sticks, she used her flint and tinder. The fire caught fast. Redlynn sat against her shelter and pulled an apple from her pocket. She unsheathed a hunting knife from her boot and peeled off the skin. She played and replayed the events of Anya's cleansing in her mind.

A tear slipped from her eye and dribbled down her cheek. Cutting a piece of an apple Yanti had given her, she closed her eyes and shook her head to clear it. *I've done cleansings a dozen times. And if I kill the King of the Weres, I won't have to do them again.*

The hours dragged on and the temperature dropped rapidly. Redlynn pulled her cloak tighter, exhausted from the events of the last twenty-four hours. But the anticipation of a fight left her antsy, despite her weary state.

She grabbed two logs from the pile she'd collected; she threw them in the pit and slipped into her hollow. Curling up in her bedroll, she covered herself with her cloak. She stared at the fire, bleary-eyed.

Over the last five years she'd watched Sisters find men and settle down, taking them out of active membership in the Sisterhood. Or leave the village, never to be heard from again.

Just once, she wished that she'd find someone who looked at her with affection, instead of turning away from her like she was

18

deformed. Maybe if she moved to a different village, and got a fresh start, she'd find a place where she fit in and belonged. Possibly in the farmlands, or in Westfall. She could start an apothecary like her mother used to have.

Redlynn blinked slowly, uneasiness scratched up her spine. Silence permeated the air, but for the roaring fire. She sat up and pushed out of the tree. The crickets no longer chirped, and no animals rustled.

Wind blew the smoke from the campfire in her direction and she coughed lightly. She stood and strapped on her sword. Her skin prickled. Redlynn scanned the surrounding area, her heart thudding in her chest. The crackles and pops of the logs on the fire sounded abnormally loud in the silence.

A faint rustle emanated from the bushes on the other side of the fire. She grabbed her bow, notching an arrow. Calming her breathing, she strained to see into the blackness beyond the glow. *This is it. What you've been waiting for your whole life, to become a hunter.*

Crunching sounded from behind her, and she spun around, aiming at the unseen assailant. A snap came from the other direction and she spun back. *Keep it together!* Redlynn breathed deep and remembered her training. She backed into the tree she'd been hiding in, not allowing herself to be surrounded.

I can get off three shots.

A Were broke through the darkness directly across from her, a guttural growl escaping the beast's chest. Twice the size of a normal wolf, it stood five feet at the shoulders. Its golden fur glistened in the firelight. Her palms were slick as she let her first arrow fly. *One.* It caught the Were in the shoulder and the wolf released an anguished howl. The beast's chocolate eyes trained on Redlynn. Several other Weres entered the clearing, circling about her. Pulling another arrow, she shot again at the golden Were. *Two.* He bared his teeth and batted it away with the swipe of a paw.

19

A grey Were lunged, and she swung her bow, striking it on the nose. The animal yelped, stumbled and hit a log from the fire, sending it across the ground, snapping and spitting. The Weres stepped away, watching her. She loosed another arrow, but the Weres moved out of the way easily and it sailed off into the trees. *Three. Crap.*

They were toying with her.

"Enough games," she yelled, throwing her bow to the ground and taking off her long cloak. Her mind calculated the best option for attack. Unsheathing her sword, she swung at the grey Were, slicing into his flank. The beast yelped and stumbled, blood oozing from his wound.

Redlynn lunged at him again and thrust her sword into his side. Pulling the sword free, she swung wide and prepared to finish him, but the golden Were attacked from behind, knocking her off balance, and the Grey escaped into the woods. *Dammit!*

The golden Were knocked her to the earth, her face close to the flames. Angered by the escaped Were, Redlynn flipped herself away from the searing heat. She fumbled and lost hold of her sword. He pounced on her, pinning her to the ground with his crushing weight. Its giant maw was inches from her face, encasing her in the stench of its hot breath.

Get up! Get out from under him, her mind screamed. She reached out, grabbed the arrow still stuck in his shoulder, and tried to shove. The arrow inched deeper, making the Were yelp in pain. Lowering his mouth, he latched onto her shoulder. His ice pick-sized teeth tore into her flesh and Redlynn screamed. Pain rushed through her. Another Were rammed into the golden one, and he lost his hold on her shoulder. She needed to gain control of the situation.

Reaching for her boot, she pulled out her hunting knife and jammed it into the Were's fleshy under belly. Again, the beast latched onto her shoulder. Redlynn screamed in agony. Her bones

20

crunched as her collarbone snapped, and her left arm went limp. She had to get the beast off of her. Reaching with her right hand, she clutched the hunting knife and pulled it out, shoving it into the beast's rib cage.

The Were tumbled sideways. Rolling over, she struggled to her feet. Redlynn dropped the knife and grabbed her sword, hefting it with her right hand. Her weak grasp barely gripped the hilt. Blood poured down between her breasts and pooled at her waist, drenching her blouse. The golden Were lay on its side, unmoving. The Grey had vanished, but two more still watched her from the other side of the fire.

Her left arm hung limply at her side, useless. Pain shot through her entire body, but she refused to give in to shock. If they attacked again, she was done for. In the lull of the battle, the smell of her own blood made her woozy. She closed her eyes and swallowed hard, trying to gain her bearings. Reopening her blurry eyes, she swayed on the spot. Her sword arm fell and she struggled to lift it. She tried to formulate a plan, but her body felt heavy, and she couldn't focus.

But still the Weres didn't move.

"What are you waiting for?" she yelled.

The Weres raised their hackles and bared their teeth, but something held them at bay.

Oh no! There was no way she was going to let them wait till she was unconscious to finish her off. If they wanted her dead, they were going to have to fight for it.

Gathering her remaining strength, she charged. Her sword raised, she ran past the fire straight at the two animals. Redlynn swung wild, barely controlling the sword. The Weres jumped out of her way and she missed them both. She had to choose. Lunging at the one on her right, she stabbed with her sword. The Were dodged and then reared back on his haunches before springing at her, knocking her into a tree. Redlynn twisted her body and hit the

21

thick trunk with a whack. Pain pounded through her temple. Everything went fuzzy, and then black.

CHAPTER THREE

"What happened to her?" Adrian demanded, bounding through the trees toward the smoke of the campfire.

"She attacked us, my Lord. Dominic is dead, Paulo is badly injured."

"Wait for me and don't touch her. I'm on my way," he growled.

A female. A human female, in the woods. There hadn't been one in almost five years. Adrian needed to get to her before his men did any more damage, or before something worse found her.

Rushing through the woods, he caught the scent of the animals hiding in their homes. Adrian loved the run. He loved the freedom of it. At the castle, there was nothing to do but fend off the bloodsuckers and exist.

Females were precious, and Weres were forbidden from harming them, no matter what they did. If Dominic were dead, he deserved it. The scent of smoke grew stronger, and he glimpsed a flicker of light in the distance. He loped over a fallen tree and spotted a thick grove of eldergreens. Bursting through them, he came upon the small cove.

Adrian surveyed the scene and began to shift. Dominic lay on his side next to a blazing fire. Blain, Chrisio and Juda stood near the unconscious female. Forcing his form into its human shape, his bones snapped, his feet flattened. With the cracking of his knuckles, his fingers lengthened. The muscles of his spine pulled tight and forced him to stand on his feet. He sneezed as his nose flattened and his teeth retracted. The hair of his body shortened, revealing his skin, covered in a fine layer of sweat.

Blain had his palm on the girl's forehead. Juda and Chrisio backed away from the female as Adrian stepped toward her.

"What happened?" he demanded.

Blain stood. "I caught the end of it. By the time I got here, Dominic was barely breathing, and Paulo had fled."

Adrian neared the girl slumped by the tree, her flowing red hair covering her face. He brushed back a thick strand to reveal soft skin, the color of peaches. Her lips curved like a bow, pale as a pink rose. The sight of her set him on fire. High and thin cheekbones framed her small pixie nose perfectly. His gut clenched and the hair stood up on his arms. The scent of her hit him in a wave that coursed through his body and made him step away from her.

His gaze whipped toward Blain. "Have you scented her? She's different."

"She smells like any other female." Blain shrugged.

He turned to the unconscious girl, his senses on overdrive from being near her. "Not to me."

Though bloody and dirty, she was the most beautiful woman he'd ever seen. His inner wolf begged to be near her. A need lit within him, the likes of which Adrian had never felt. He blinked several times. What is this? This sudden rush of emotions he had for a female he didn't even know the name of. Adrian scowled. No. There was no way he was getting close to a Sister.

He moved to her side and gently slid her onto her back. Assessing the wounds, a ripple of anger tore through him, and his gaze darted to Dominic's lifeless corpse. He growled and bared his teeth, wishing more than anything that Dominic were still alive so he could rip him to pieces for what he'd done.

A gaping tear in her neck bled heavily. Her shoulder lay at an odd angle, her collarbone broken. It was possible the upper arm bone was broken as well.

"Find some fernblend." Adrian placed his hand over the wound to try and staunch the flow.

"Of course, my Lord," said Chrisio.

He looked around for something to use for pressure. "Give me that cloak." He pointed.

"What'll we do with her?" Juda picked up the cloak and handed it over.

The things that Adrian wanted to do with her were not something he wished to discuss. What he should do was another matter all together. Adrian shook his head again, trying to clear her scent out of his nose. Come on. Pull it together.

"We'll take her with us, like all the others." He used the edge of the cloak to put pressure on the wound.

"We should deliver her to Volkzene. Let them heal her," Blain suggested. "I don't think she'll take kindly to us."

Yes. We should take her back. "What goodwill do you think the Sisters will show us if we bring her to the village, having been attacked by a wolf? To do so would make the rift between us and them even worse."

Blain opened his mouth to speak, but then shut it. "Good point."

"We take her with us." Adrian's gut clenched again. It was a bad idea.

Juda stood apart from the group, his jaw set.

"I have the fernblend, Sire." Chrisio held out the leaves.

Adrian took the handful of small dark foliage and bruised it between his palms. Tearing and rubbing the leaves, he ground them into a wad, and then mixed them with his saliva. Removing the cloak, he ripped at her shirt and exposed the wound. Adrian stopped to admire the peachy flesh and round curves of her ample breast. His breath caught in his throat.

"What the–" Blain peered over Adrian's shoulder. "Is that–"

A tremor coursed through Adrian's body. His Alpha wanted out. A female with the mark had been born. They'd waited for hundreds of years for the prophecy to be fulfilled. Adrian backed away from her quickly. It wasn't possible.

"Adrian–"

"You, Chrisio and Juda take Dominic's body to the castle. Bring clothes for me and a horse." Adrian's need to get the men away from her overwhelmed him. His chest tightened and his heart thundered. He didn't want this. Not now.

His men moved off without a word. He stared down at her, not wanting to touch her. She was a member of the Sisterhood, and he had made a promise to keep them safe. Kneeling, he continued working the wad of leaves into the exposed flesh. She didn't stir. The pain of the leaves should have at least caused her to rouse. He snatched up the cloak and ripped a long strip off the bottom. Taking the strip, he threaded it around her back and over her breast, then moving her arm across her body, he tied the strip tight, pinning her arm in place.

When he was done, he tried to arrange her comfortably. He shut her tunic and covered her with the cloak. Walking around, he tried to piece together the scene, trying to make sense of what had happened. Blood spattered the ground and nearby trees. If there were bloodsuckers in the woods, they'd be drawn to the scent. He hoped Blain returned soon.

He found her bedroll, pack, bow, quiver and sword. Pulling them all together, he laid them near her, and then sat down next to her to wait. The ground was cold beneath his bare legs, but he was used to it. Staring down at her, he wondered what color her eyes were. Green would be his assumption, considering her complexion. He plucked a leaf from her red hair and his heartbeat quickened.

Leaning in close to her, he smelled her again. It was earthy and woodsy, smelling faintly of rosemary. The scent soothed his pain, eased his loneliness, and made his wolf sit up and want to be obedient. Stop! Adrian pushed his wolf down. He'd been alone for so many years, as had his father before him, and over half the wolves in his kingdom. They paid for the mistakes of his father by protecting the humans from the bloodsuckers in the kingdom to the north. Waiting out the days until the prophecy was fulfilled and the bloodshed would be over.

One will be born, with the mark of the wolf, to the Sisterhood of Red.
And when she finds her destiny, the bloodshed she will end.
Taken to bed, by the mate of her soul, a reminder she will be.
And then will the females follow her home, the cursed will be set free.

Adrian glanced down at her covered breast, where the mark sat upon her skin. His wolf's protectiveness stirred within, and he set her hair back in place. It was all he could do to stop himself from pulling down her blouse once more, just to make sure he hadn't imagined it. His body tingled at the nearness of her. He scooted sideways away from her.

Blain returned with two horses and a set of clothing. He packed her things while Adrian tugged on his clothes. Something shiny on the ground caught Adrian's eye by a hollow tree. He picked up the gold necklace and fingered the locket before putting it in his saddlebag.

"Would you like me to help you with her?" Blain asked.

"No," Adrian said too quickly. He cleared his throat, commanding his inner wolf to back away. "I'll get her." But he wouldn't be able to mount the horse while carrying her. Taking a deep breath, he locked eyes with Blain. "Lift her to me, please."

Blain nodded with a smirk.

"Don't give me that look."

27

Blain laughed lightly.

He threw his foot into the stirrup and hefted himself up onto Montego, his steed. Settling into the saddle, Blain held the girl.

"Be careful of her arm." He tried to keep his temper in check.

"I am." Blain shook his head, hoisted the girl up, and at the last minute stopped. "Are you sure you want to carry her? I wouldn't mind."

"Give her to me," Adrian growled.

"I'm joking. What's wrong with you?"

Adrian didn't know what was wrong. For all of his not wanting anything to do with her, he didn't want Blain touching her, either. "Just give her to me. We need to get her out of the woods."

Blain eyed Adrian, but Adrian ignored him. He needed the safety of the castle. The longer they were out, the more anxious he became. If the bloodsuckers struck, they'd be lucky to make it out alive.

Adrian gazed at the girl. The way her body curled into his. She lay cool against his chest, weighing so little in his arms. His body relaxed into her, despite his efforts to stay strong. She murmured something, but he couldn't make it out. The scent of her flaming hair swirled in his nostrils. With her now in his arms, the scent overpowered him. Slapping his reins, Adrian got Montego moving.

They'd been making their way through the forest for several minutes when Blain broke through his thoughts.

"She tried to kill us."

"They all try at first. She's no different. It's not their fault that my mother chose to lead the Sisterhood astray."

"You think she's the one. Don't you?"

Adrian swallowed. "I don't think anything."

"You lie, Adrian. I know you too well. Look how you sit with her in your arms. As Prince you could have taken any of the females that came to us to mate. But you've not so much as looked twice at any of them till now."

The silence fell between them as they rode for several miles. Adrian had no need of a female. He was happy where he was. If he took a mate, he'd become King. He had no intention of ever doing that.

"How many years have we waited?" Blain asked. "For the Sisterhood to return to us, and the war with the bloodsuckers to end?"

"We'll continue on the path that my father set us on before his death. We will continue to make penance for the betrayal he rendered my mother. And if this is the girl from the prophecy, then you will all be blessed when more Sisters come."

"Adrian you know that the prophecy says–"

"I do. Now can you just shut it, please?"

They rode the rest of the way in silence. When the moon shone through the trees, Adrian stole glances at the exquisite beauty in his arms. Inwardly he prayed that she'd break the curse and bring an end to the war. His wolves were sick of being the fodder in the battle. But he'd do whatever it took to keep the Sisterhood of Red safe. Not because of any budding attraction, but because of his promise.

CHAPTER FOUR

The site of his castle never ceased to be both a comfort and prison to Adrian. His fortress of protection was the place he'd been raised by his mother and father as a young boy, and the last refuge for his wolves.

They'd made it back, unmolested. A sense of relief washed over him seeing the turrets, along with the grey stone battlements, come into view. Sentinels stood watch in the light towers, on the four corners of the structure. The portcullis was up and the drawbridge lay flat across the moat, awaiting his return. The sound of Montego's hooves on the wooden planks was a welcome sound.

The scent of the blacksmith's smoke tickled his nose. The sounds of Angus' hammering on the forge pounded in his head. Two of his men pulled a hide onto a tanning rack, preparing it. A female sat watching her young ones play as she worked on her needlepoint.

Several men moved out of his path, and then stopped, staring at the woman he carried across the courtyard. Adrian clenched his jaw to keep himself from spewing angry words at them. It wasn't their fault that they watched her with hopeful eyes; they all craved the affection of a mate. Word would spread quickly that another female had been found.

A female suckling her infant looked up from where she sat.

"Female." Adrian slowed his horse.

"Darina, Highness." The woman stood and bowed.

"Darina. Please fetch Hanna and tell her to bring her herbs to my quarters."

The woman's gaze drifted to the female in his arms. "Of course, your Highness." She swaddled her baby and moved swiftly for the castle.

He pulled his horse up to the stable and waited for Blain to dismount. Lash exited the stables and took hold of the reins for both steeds. His gaze never left the sleeping girl.

"Can I?" Blain held his arms out to take her.

Adrian tensed, but let her slide from his grasp. He hated that he was so protective of a female he didn't even know. Jumping from his horse, he took the girl's limp body in his arms and stalked toward the castle. His heavy boots clunked on the stone floor as he made his way through the entrance hall. Dax waited for him, speaking to Blain. Both men turned and looked at Adrian approaching.

"Dax," said Adrian. "Please take this female to my room." Adrian handed the female over to the large shifter.

Dax took her gently into his arms and headed for the stairs. Adrian's gaze followed them.

"I'm going to grab Jale and Juda and go back out," said Blain.

Adrian turned. "We didn't spot any vampires tonight. There's no need to go back out."

Blain nodded. "True, but we've seen that tall blond one coming and going more often, and after the last encounter, I owe him." Blain's eyes travelled up the stairs. "Besides, I could use some air."

Adrian wished he could go out for some air. But he needed to make sure the female was safe, and that Hannah visited her. "Send Jale back if you find the vampire. I want to question him before we kill him."

Blain smiled. "I'll do my best to keep him alive. Mostly."

The two large, dark-haired males stalked into the entrance hall. Adrian tensed at the sight of them. Jale and Juda nodded to Adrian.

"Heard there's a new female," said Jale.

"Yes," Adrian crossed his arms over his chest. There was no way in hell he was going to let either of them anywhere near her.

Adrian took the stairs to his room, two at a time. Dax opened the door, letting him in.

"Has she stirred?"

Dax shook his heavy blond head.

Adrian moved to his large four-poster bed, raised on a pedestal in the middle of his room, and stared at the girl. Her hair fanned out around her in a deep red halo. Her skin had lost its peachy color and had taken on a more waxen sheen. Reaching down, he wrapped her red cloak over her to keep her warm. She looked small and helpless in his bed. Her lean frame seemed to take up no space at all. Why had he told Dax to bring her here? She should have been put down with the other women.

"Is she one of the Sisterhood?" Dax asked.

"Most likely."

Dax moved to the side of the bed and laid his large palm on her forehead. "Vampires?"

"Dominic." Adrian gritted his teeth. His Alpha wolf was getting anxious about Dax touching her. The werebear was not technically one of his pack. Dax had been adopted in when he'd shown up, half-dead and with no memory, almost three years prior.

"That explains a lot." Dax shook his head. "Paulo will heal."

Adrian nodded, but wasn't listening. He watched the simple rise and fall of her chest. *Her breathing's strong, which is a good sign.* "Where the hell is Hanna?" he fumed.

"I'm here, your highness." Hanna stepped into the room.

"Good." Adrian motioned her to the bed.

"I'll find you something to eat." Dax exited.

Hanna looked down at the girl. "Oh my, it's Red!" She hastily threw her bag to the floor and removed Redlynn's cloak. "What happened to her?"

Hanna's eyes turned to Adrian, but he dare not tell her the truth. "You know her then?"

"Her full name is Redlynn. Her ancestors took over as Heads of the Order after your mother passed. She was young when I left, maybe only thirteen."

"And her parents?"

"She had a hard life before her father disappeared." Hanna pulled items out of her bag, setting them on the nightstand. "Her mother tried to tell the truth about the Sisters being wolf mates. I'm not sure how she found out."

"What happened to her?"

"She was denounced. The council assumed her husband's disappearance caused a mental break. She was never the same after that."

Hanna removed the strip of cloak tying Redlynn's arm to her side, and pulled down her blouse.

"M'lord!" Hanna looked over her shoulder at him. "She has the mark."

"I know," Adrian replied.

"But that means–" A smile spread across Hanna's face as she clasped her hands together and raised her gaze to the heavens. "The gods be praised. The time has come when we'll all be reunited."

The gods have nothing to do with it. Adrian had long given up on the idea of the gods stepping in to help any of them.

Hanna pulled Redlynn's blouse open further, inspecting the wound. "I'm sorry to ask you M'lord, but I need water and a towel, so I may remove some of the blood."

"I'll do it." Adrian moved swiftly into the adjoining bathing room and took a deep breath. His mind raced once again with

33

thoughts of what he wished he could do to Dominic for hurting Red. He stood in the doorway, unable to remember why he was in there. A beautiful, half-naked woman lay in his bed. He'd never had a woman in his bed before. *Think! Why did you come in here? Water! Towel!*

He grabbed the items Hanna had asked for and took them out to her, averting his eyes. Several minutes passed, and there was a moan from the bed. He turned and caught a glimpse of a perfectly rounded breast. He turned away again. "Is she alright?"

"The wound is deep and fernblend has dried into it. I'll apply a clean dressing and some salve to help stave off infection. Her shoulder appears to be at an odd angle, but until I can inspect her further I won't know the extent of her injuries. She needs rest. I can have her moved–"

"She'll stay here, I have a dozen rooms in this wing to choose from." He should just tell Hanna to take Red down to the other wing. He had no interest in becoming attached to her. Especially since he had no intention on being the one she chose.

Hanna's face softened and she gave him a knowing look. "That'd be best, M'lord. I'll return in the morning."

Adrian glanced at the painting above the fireplace: his mother, Irina, with her long raven hair, and his father, Sven, standing proudly beside her. For a fleeting moment, he ached for his mother's comfort and his father's wise counsel. Long had it been since he'd heard his parents' voices.

It wouldn't matter, Adrian thought, looking into his mother's face. *She was the one who did this in the first place.* He ran his hands over his face and hair, trying to forget the ghosts of his past.

He turned to the bed. Hanna had secured Redlynn's arm. She picked up the bowl of blood-tinged water and towels and her bag. Tenderness crossed her soft face. "I'll bring her some clothing when I return. Tomorrow she needs to bathe."

"She has a bag. I don't know what is in it, though. Blain has it."

"I'll get that as well, then."

"Thank you, Hanna. Tell your mate, Fendrick, I appreciate his letting me borrow you."

Hanna laughed to herself and nodded. "I'll be sure to let him know. Good night, your highness."

"Adrian."

Hanna hesitated, and then nodded. "Prince Adrian."

*****

Redlynn whipped her head from side to side. *Where am I?* Pain exploded in her neck; she tried to reach up with her left arm, but it was pinned to her stomach. It'd been strapped in place by a strip of red cloth. *Why am I half-naked?* Her tunic and cloak were gone. So was her locket. Redlynn looked around frantically for her locket. Pain hit her in waves, confusing her and forcing her to breathe deeply. She refused to cry.

Trying to process her surroundings, the fight with the Were flooded back to her. Shockingly, it seemed she wasn't dead, she was alive, and in someone's very richly furnished bedroom. She wiped at her face with her right hand, her vision muddled.

Stone walls surrounded the large, mahogany, four-poster bed she lay upon. Dark, heavy curtains were partially drawn at the end of the bed. On either side, two ancient and beautiful nightstands held ornately carved glass oil lamps. A fire crackled, its golden glow peeking in the gaps of the curtains.

Redlynn maneuvered herself to the side of the bed and set her feet on the floor. It was colder than her wooden planks at home. Slowly she scooted off the downy mattress, and tried to steady herself on one of the posts. She weakened, the blood draining from her head, her legs wobbling beneath her.

On the floor lay her cloak. She stooped to pick it up, but lost her balance. At the last minute, she braced herself on the stone wall

35

and avoided its colliding with her face. Taking a deep breath, she steadied herself once more and slowly reached down for the cloak, pressing herself into the stone for support. It took her several minutes to get the clasps buckled so that she was covered almost to her waist.

By the time she finished, her body shook like she'd tried to pull a wagon by herself. A bead of sweat trickled down the side of her face. Sucking in a deep breath, she tried to clear her mind and listen for sounds. A faint rhythmical buzzing came from somewhere near the fire. Pushing past the end of the bed, she saw a large man asleep at a table.

His head was tilted to the side and long, wavy black hair fell over his eyes and chiseled features. His large and strong form was set with broad shoulders and a powerfully built frame. He'd fallen asleep in his linen shirt and breeches, with his boots still on. A flutter settled in her stomach, the same surge of adrenaline she got before a fight. He was snoring. What was he doing there?

Confused, Redlynn wasn't sure if it was her fighting instincts kicking in, or something else all together. Part of her wanted to know what his lips would feel like on hers. Another part wanted to run.

What the hell is wrong with you? You'd think you'd never seen a man before. She swallowed hard. She hadn't. *Not a man like him.*

She searched for an exit and found it to the far left of the room. The sleeping man didn't look like he was guarding her, but why would he be in the same room with her, if he weren't? She scanned the room for her things. Her pack, bow and quiver were nowhere to be found. If she were going to break out, she needed a weapon.

On the table lay a tray with an empty plate, a knife, fork and spoon. Redlynn inched toward the knife. The closer she got to him, the more drawn she was to him. She stopped, a foot from the table.

Keep it together! He's only a man, and obviously your guard.
For all you know, he could be a murderer!

She slid her good hand across the polished wooden surface. As she reached for the knife, her collarbone burned with pain. She stumbled, tripping over her cloak and crashing into the plate.

The man was up in an instant. Rising, his chair clattered to the ground. Redlynn grabbed hold of the knife and held it out in front of herself, backing away. It took him a moment to comprehend what was going on. He stared at her, not moving. She shook like a rabbit. He had golden eyes.

"Your... your eyes," she whispered.

"What's wrong with them?"

"They... They're gold."

"They're brown."

"No. No, they aren't." She shook her head. "They're golden... just like–"

"Like yours," he murmured.

Redlynn nodded, her head fuzzy, and her knees wobbly. She blinked several times. His eyes were brown. They had golden flecks in them, but they were definitely brown.

"You've had a bad wound. You should rest."

"I have to leave. I have something I need to do."

"Do you remember what happened?"

"Where am I?"

"In Wolvenglen."

"Who in their right mind would live in Wolvenglen? Don't you know there are Weres out here?"

"Please, put down the knife." He motioned to the knife Redlynn had forgotten she was pointing at him.

She glanced at it and weighed it in her hand. It was solid. Her hunting knife was larger, but she could make do with it if need be.

"Where are my things? I need to go."

37

"Hanna, our healer, will bring them in the morning when she comes to check on you, and bring you a change of clothes."

Still holding the knife, she reached up and touched her collarbone, underneath her cloak. A bandage covered the wound. It was tender. Peeling it away, she assessed what she could see of the damage.

"I wouldn't do that," he warned.

Redlynn gave him a hard stare and went back to inspecting the wound. She stuck her fingers in the salve and rolled it between her thumb and forefinger, smelling it.

"Comfrey and calendula." Pulling at the green leaves, she winced as they ripped a piece of skin and seeped. Smelling the leaves, she put them in her mouth and chewed them before spitting them out. "Fernblend. Did she do that?"

"No, I did."

"Don't you know you have to keep it wet?"

"I thought saving your life was more important," he bit back. "You were in bad shape when I found you."

"Well when I scrub it off, I am going to wish I were dead. Where did you find me, anyway?"

"Listen." He took a deep breath. His eyes softened and his voice gentled. "I was trying to help you. It was one of the few things I remember my mother teaching me about herbs."

"Your mother's a healer?"

"Was. Now, will you please lie down before you pass out? You lost a lot of blood."

"I've had worse," Redlynn lied. "I need to get my things and be on my way."

"You need to rest. You can barely hold that knife, let alone walk through the forest."

"I'll be fine."

He stepped out of her way. "Very well. You are free to leave." He motioned to the door.

38

Was this a joke? Was he really going to let her go? Gripping the knife, she took several steady steps toward the exit before her knees buckled. He caught her around the waist, sending a shockwave of tingles through her body.

His musky scent mixed in her nostrils and her head lightened again. His body wasn't just warm, it was hot; he was a fire in his own right.

"Let go," she said softly.

"I was merely keeping you from further injuring yourself."

His light blue tunic opened in a "v" and his chiseled, hairless chest peaked out beneath. Her eyes locked with his. He hadn't shaved in a day or two; the whiskers looked ruggedly good on him. His face wore an expression she'd never seen aimed at her before. Desire. The butterflies in her stomach danced and spun. His face was so close as he studied her features.

"Please, let go," she choked, her voice raw with tension.

He continued to stare at her for a moment more, and then swooped her into his arms as if she were a child. She stiffened at the press of his body against hers.

Her heart thundered in her chest. A man had never held her before. "Let go of me." She pushed at his chest and tried to twist from his grip. The movement made her dizzy again.

"Stop, before I drop you," he said. He pushed the curtains aside, and laid her where she'd started.

Redlynn's mind whirled as she lay on the bed. The scent of his skin lingered near her. She swallowed hard. He'd touched her. No man had ever wanted to touch her before.

Prying the knife from her hand, he set it on the nightstand and stepped away. "You have no need of a weapon here. No one will hurt you. I promise."

He stood feet away, but oddly it felt too far. Her reaction to him made no sense, but she wanted him holding her, in the large bed. She said nothing. Stepping forward again, he pulled the sheet and coverlet over her. She shrunk away from his touch.

"I won't hurt you."

"How do I know that? Here I am in a strange house, in someone else's bed, no less."

"Because you have my word."

"And what is that to me? I don't know you." She should be grateful for being saved from the wolves, but being in a place where she didn't know anyone set her on edge. She'd never seen such finery.

A slight smile played on his lips. "You must be thirsty. I'll get you a drink."

If he left, she might be able to escape.

"But only if you promise not to try and leave again."

Her gaze met his and her eyes narrowed. How had he known? She wanted to get out and get back to her task at hand. The Weres needed to pay for the pain they'd caused. She shifted her position and her arm shot a pain up the side of her neck. "I'll wait till after your healer arrives."

His eyes searched hers. He nodded, and then turned to leave and paused, pulling something from his pocket. "I found this, is it yours?" He held up the locket.

Relief flooded her. He'd found it! She reached out with her good arm. "Thank you. It was my mother's."

He stepped in close before she could protest and refastened the clasp behind her neck. "I had a new clasp put on it for you."

She inhaled his soothing musky scent. She swallowed hard. He was touching her again. When he stepped away she said, "Thank you. It was the only thing my father ever gave her. In all my life, I'd never seen her take it off. I almost let them burn her with it, but in the end, I just couldn't." Redlynn ran her fingers over the locket engraved with a Volkzene flower.

40

"My father once gave my mother something similar. She said it was her most prized possession. She used to carry around a lock of my hair and my father's hair in it."

He watched her for a moment with an expression she couldn't read, and then walked out of the room.

After he was gone, she took a deep breath. What the hell was that? She hadn't even asked him who he was. Lying down on the pillow, Redlynn closed her eyes. His scent lingered on the pillows. The bed had to be his. Panic stirred inside her. What if his plan was to try and force her into sex? She eyed the knife he'd taken from her, and then grabbed it and pulled it under her cape. He'd said no one would hurt her, but who was he? Why should she trust his word?

But his eyes. His deep brown eyes had held desire for her, when he'd caught her. And he smelled so good. Just the thought of his tightly bunched muscles surrounding her and carrying her to the bed was enough to make her want more. Somehow when he touched her, all she'd wanted was more. Warmth between her legs that was both uncomfortable, and begging to be satisfied. She twitched in her breeches and rubbed her thighs together. Redlynn grumbled. That was not helping.

It's the blood loss, she decided. *It had to be.* No woman in her right mind, especially this woman, would ever want a man at first sight.

Sucking in a deep breath, she gripped the handle of the knife tightly. Tomorrow would be different. She'd be on her way. Back to the forest to hunt the beasts she'd come for, and leave all thoughts and desires for her captor behind.

CHAPTER FIVE

Her eyes are gold. Adrian couldn't wrap his head around it. Her eyes were golden like his, when he changed. How was it possible? And how was it that they were golden? Obviously it was a trick of the light. It meant nothing. But the way she'd looked at him; so desperate, and defiant, but no fear. He would've smelled her fear. She was strong. The strongest he'd met. And full of pain, both physical and emotional.

Adrian rushed down the stairs to the kitchen. She needed liquid and food, something to nourish her. He wished he could find her something that he'd killed himself for her to eat, but there was no time. He stopped abruptly. What if she lied? What if she's sneaking out to the forest right now? *Stop it!* What was wrong with him? She was a female. So what. He moved again, slower this time. He'd refused every other female that had shown up on the castle steps. He refused to take a mate and become king. He wouldn't allow himself to be broken the way his father had.

But when he'd caught her in his arms, the connection had sent chills up his neck and warmth through his thighs. His inner wolf was alive for the first time, and it only wanted her.

He passed through the dining hall. It was sparse at the late hour, except for a few of the older pack members. Angus, a close friend of his father's, stared at his mug of ale, as several others joked and told stories.

"Prince Adrian." Angus nodded.

"Evening, Angus. And you know it's just 'Adrian.'"

"Heard there was a new female."

"Yes. A member of the Sisterhood. Her name is Red."

Angus breathed deeply and his eyes widened. He breathed in again, his eyes scanning the room.

Adrian looked around. "Something wrong?"

Angus stared at him mutely, and then went back to his mug of ale. "Nope."

Adrian's heart went out to Angus. To have lived so long and still he hadn't found a mate.

Entering the kitchen, Adrian was surprised to find the wooden table full of food. Jale and his brother Juda sat hunched over in a low conversation. Upon spotting Adrian, they went silent. He stood in the doorway, watching the pair. Jale and Juda made no bones about telling everyone who would listen their views on his refusal to go to the Sisterhood and reclaim them. He'd have thrown them out years ago, but to do so would mean their death sentence. There was nowhere else for them to go.

Adrian grabbed a platter from a shelf and headed for the larder. "Jale. Juda." He acknowledged them with a nod.

"Adrian," they replied in turn.

Inside, Adrian found cheese, grapes, bread, mead and dried meat. He piled them high on the platter and turned to leave.

"That girl gonna live?" Juda bit into a piece of chicken.

Adrian stopped moving. The hairs on his neck stood on end. "She'll be fine in a few days."

"Well, that's good. Means one of us might get the chance at some happiness," Jale said.

"Not many chances come into the woods for us anymore," Juda finished.

Adrian gritted his teeth but refused to answer them. It was always the same with those two. Every male in his pack had

43

suffered at one time or another from loneliness. It was true that in the years since the Sisterhood had abandoned them, only a handful had returned, but Jale and Juda made it seem like they were the only ones.

Grabbing a goblet, fork, and knife, he walked out of the kitchen and almost smashed into Dax.

"You hungry again already?" Dax asked.

"It's not for me. But be warned, Jale and Juda are in there."

Dax's gaze shifted to the kitchen. "They givin' you any trouble?"

"No more than usual."

"I can take care of that problem for you."

Adrian laughed lightly. "Thank you, my friend, not today."

Dax nodded. "Whenever you need it dealt with, I'm there."

"I'll see you in the morning." Adrian gave him a slight smile. Dax was a good man. It was too bad he had no idea who he was.

*****

The door opened with a creak and Redlynn tried to sit up. It was more difficult than she would've thought. Her sudden attempt at escape had weakened her, and possibly done more damage, and she was paying for it now. She wished she had her bag and some white willow bark for the pain. She clutched the knife tightly from under her cloak.

The curtain pulled aside. He held a large tray piled high with food. Easing the tray onto the bed, he pushed it toward her. She'd never seen that much food at a meal in her life. Again she tried to sit up, but was unable. He moved in to help her, but she stiffened.

"I can do it."

He folded his sinewy arms across his broad chest and a small smile played on his lips. After watching her struggle for several minutes, he threaded his arm behind her, lifting her into a sitting position without asking. She clutched the knife tightly, ready to strike if he did anything inappropriate.

44

His gaze travelled to her cloak and then back to her face. "I'm sure you could've managed, but I figured you wanted to eat before morning."

Redlynn relaxed a bit. The nearness of him caused her to warm again.

"Thank you."

He walked to the foot of the bed and pushed the tray of food up next to her good hand, and then spread out on the other side of the bed.

She eyed the fork. There was no way she'd be able to feed herself with her cloak buttoned. But she wasn't about to bare herself in front of him either.

"Would you like me to feed you?" His voice was husky. She gave him a stern look and he lifted his hands. "Right, you can do it. I forgot." Adrian rolled on his back and stared at the ceiling.

Red watched him, not sure if he were making fun of her or not.

"I'm Redlynn."

"Redlynn. Good name."

She slipped the knife into her left, reached out, and grabbed the bottle of mead. She tried to pour it into the goblet, but the heavy bottle wobbled in her grip. He glanced over, and just as he lifted his hand to help, she put the bottle to her lips, taking several long draws from it.

The liquid was warm and sweet going down. After several swallows, she put it on the platter and took a deep breath.

"I was named after my great, great, great, grandmother."

"I was named after no one."

She sensed that he was trying to be funny, but it was awkward.

She picked up the bread and ripped a hunk off with her teeth, then bit a piece off the cheese and shoved it in her mouth. It tasted wonderful. She moaned at the taste of the crusty loaf.

"You must like bread," Adrian mused.

Redlynn stopped chewing. He still stared at the ceiling. "I haven't had bread since my mother died." Why had she told him that? She didn't know him.

Adrian's eyebrows knit together.

She shrugged. "I'm not very domestic."

"You don't trade with the baker in your village?"

"I'm not very social, either."

He chuckled. "Could have fooled me."

She picked up the knife and made a stab at cutting the meat. The knife stuck and she couldn't get it to release. Adrian reached over and placed his hand on top of hers, pulling the knife out. The warmth of his touch tingled and she jerked away from the sensation. She didn't like the way he made her feel.

He cut the meat for her, stuck a large piece on the end and held it out to her.

"How did you find me in the woods?" She reached for more bread.

"I smelled smoke and saw the fire while on patrol."

"Do you patrol against the Weres?"

He stared at her for a moment before answering. "We patrol against the beasts of the forest."

"Why do you live out here in Wolvenglen if it's so dangerous? Why do you and your family not live in the farmlands?"

Adrian shrugged. "I'm not a farmer."

She stabbed at another piece of meat. "If you aren't a farmer what are you? You seem to be doing well here in Wolvenglen, from the finery of this room. Are you a trader?"

"Sometimes, but not often. We like to keep to ourselves up here."

"Obviously. I hadn't even known this was here and I thought I'd been everywhere in this forest."

"We're pretty secluded. Unless you know where you're going, it can be tricky to find. When I was a boy my father took me out on a hunting trip. I got lost on the way back. At least I thought I had. Apparently it was a test. My father was only ever a dozen yards away, but I didn't know that. It took me two days, but I made it back. I'd never been so happy to see this place."

"Two days? Your father left you alone for two day in the forest?"

He shrugged. "Like I said, he didn't leave me. He could see me the entire time. It wasn't so bad. I've always been fine in the woods. I found a tree to sleep in and caught game to eat. I wasn't even scared, frustrated more than anything. He told me that when his father tested him, it had taken him five days to find his way home." He smiled.

"So if you aren't a trader, or a farmer what do you do all day?"

"Hunt, fish, read, whatever I feel like."

What ever he felt like? "But how do you keep yourself and your household?"

He snorted. "That's a bit forward of you isn't it? To ask me how I make my money."

"I've never been accused of being demure." She chewed another piece of meat.

"In Wolvenglen we all work together for the betterment of everyone."

"I don't follow."

"In Volkzene everyone has a profession do they not?"

She nodded.

"Here we don't. We all help cook, or clean, or hunt. We all fish and take care of the horses. We work together."

"How do you make money then? To pay for the things you need?"

"We have money enough to buy what we can't make ourselves, but that's very little. Here we don't barter for coins."

Money was everything in Volkzene. Those with the most, got the most respect. Like Lilith. Yanti's words about Lilith's mirror and jewels floated back to her.

"It would be interesting to live in a place that doesn't value money above all else. Probably because I've never had any."

"You grew up poor then?"

Redlynn shrugged. "My father was a terrible farmer and my mother was a healer. It was enough to put boots on my feet and food in my belly, but not much else."

"But your weapons are well made."

"They belonged to my grandmother. The sword fits me well enough, but the bow took some getting used to. And the string had to be replaced. I've learned to work it now though. Which weapon do you prefer when you hunt?"

Adrian pressed the pad of his thumb into his canine and thought for a moment. "I suppose sharp weapons are my specialty."

"Swords then?"

"Of sorts. I try to keep things as natural as possible."

What did that mean? "I don't understand. You like to use some sort of wooden sword?"

He grabbed a piece of cheese and stuffed it in his mouth. "So, what do you do, Redlynn, since you're not domestic? Are you a healer like your mother?"

"No. I can't." She shook her head violently.

"Why not?"

"It's..." She'd never told anyone but her mother the reason. She looked over at him. Oh what did it matter? She'd be gone in a day anyway. "I can't stand the sight of blood."

He laughed.

She frowned.

48

He threw up his hands. "Sorry, I'm not trying to offend. It's just, you had a bloodied sword when we found you. If you can't stand blood, how do you use a sword?"

"Blood doesn't affect me in battle."

He cocked an eyebrow.

"I know it sounds strange, but when I'm fighting all I can think of is the fight. I don't see the blood. When I have nothing else to focus on, it overwhelms me. The scent, the color, the feel." She shivered and took a drink of mead.

"So, no healing then?"

"I *can* heal. I know everything there is to know. I just... can't. The biggest thing to be done in Volkzene is deliver babies. My mother took me once." She looked at him hard. "Once."

"Okay, no babies. Got it. So what *do* you do?"

"I am a Were hunter."

Adrian's breath caught. He was very still for a moment. "A wolf hunter? Why do you hunt werewolves?"

"I am of the Sisterhood of Red, bound to keep my village safe."

"So you aren't a hunter then?"

Redlynn bristled. "I am now. Why do you call them wolves?"

Adrian pulled off a grape and popped it in his mouth, not meeting her eye. "Because that's what they are. I didn't think the Sisterhood still hunted the wolves."

"They used to. Ever since Sister Irina founded Volkzene Village."

His gaze fixed on Redlynn. There was a sadness about them that hit her. He stared for a long time before reaching over and taking a drink from the bottle of mead. His stare made a shiver run over her.

"But they stopped hunting, didn't they?"

"Five years ago, after Lillith took over as Head of the Order, she forbade anyone to enter into the woods."

49

"Ahhhh." Adrian gave a wry smile. "So you've rebelled?"

Anger boiled in Redlynn's gut and she clenched her jaw tightly. "Two nights ago, three beasts came into my village, stole a young girl, and killed—" Redlynn dropped her gaze to the plate. She sucked in a deep breath, refusing to show weakness. "Someone dear to me," she choked.

Adrian sat straight up on the bed, his body rigid. "A girl was taken?"

"Too many have been taken in the last months. I won't stand for it any longer." Her voice hardened. "I've come to find the Weres and kill them all."

Adrian eyes drifted down at the bedspread. She felt the compulsion to take his hand, but didn't. "Have you had girls go missing, too?"

"What?" He lifted his gaze.

"The Weres. Have they taken girls from you, as well?"

"No. We've lost no one to the wolves." He seemed distracted.

"Never?" Something about his manner made Redlynn uneasy. "Have you never had any problems with the wolves? I can't believe you live in the middle of their territory, and they've never bothered you."

He stood abruptly. "Finish eating and rest."

Redlynn watched him leave. Something had upset him. He stopped and turned.

"I'll return with Hanna in the morning." Then he dipped his head and left without another word.

Redlynn spent a long time staring at the bedroom door, wondering what had rattled him. It didn't matter, it wasn't her concern. In the morning she'd meet the healer, and then be on her way.

She removed the hidden knife and shoved it under her pillow. Pushing at the tray of food with her foot, she tried to find a comfortable position to lie down in.

Adrian took the stairs two at a time down to the lower level of the castle. Someone was stealing females from Volkzene Village. Someone from his pack. He wanted to line them all up and beat every single one till they confessed. He'd find out who was doing this and why, and then he was going to rip them apart.

Upon reaching the lower level, he almost ran down the hall to the last room on the left. He tried the handle, but it was locked. He banged on the door with his fist.

"Blain. Blain!"

A muffled voice murmured inside. He pounded again and the lock slid. Blain stood naked, yawning.

"What's going on?"

"Someone's been stealing girls." Adrian burst in and pushed past his friend.

Blain rubbed his face. "Come on in," he murmured. "What time is it?"

"Did you hear me? Sisterhood females, from Volkzene. Someone from the pack is stealing girls."

Sleepiness retreated from Blain's face. "What? Who told you that?"

"Redlynn."

Blain's brows furrowed.

"The girl from the forest. She's of the Sisterhood, and came into the woods as a werewolf hunter."

"I thought the Sisterhood didn't hunt us anymore."

"She disobeyed." He grabbed his hair by the roots and tugged. This is bad. So very bad. Adrian's Alpha within howled. A ripple skittered over him and his nails lengthened.

Blain laughed. "Well, guess she won't be staying long."

"This is serious," Adrian yelled.

"I get it, Adrian. I get it." Blain sat his lean body down on his satiny bed. "Okay. Tell me exactly what she said."

"You think maybe…" Adrian gestured to Blain's nakedness.

"Huh? Oh! Really, Adrian? It isn't like you haven't seen me naked a million times, Prude." Blain pulled out a pair of breeches and tugged them on. "Better?"

"Much."

"You sure are going to make a great wife someday."

"Shut it, pup." Adrian's mood was heavy. "Redlynn said two nights ago wolves stole a girl and killed someone close to her."

"Was the someone her mate?"

A mate? He'd never thought of that. Had she said it was her mate? No, she'd said it was someone close to her. Besides I would've smelled it on her if a male had been with her.

"Is she sure it was wolves? Could it have been the bloodsuckers?"

"What?" he asked distracted.

"Stuck on the mate part, huh? I asked if she was sure it was wolves. It could've been vampires."

"We look nothing like bloodsuckers, in case you haven't noticed. We would've known if they were in the woods. Who was on patrol?"

"I was in charge of patrols that night."

Adrian rubbed his hands over his face and through his hair. This was his fault. If he took control of his pack the way he was suppose to, this never would've happened. Guilt hit him for being too selfish to mate and become king. Now he'd broken his promise to his father to keep the Sisters safe. If he'd take the throne the way his father had wanted him to, he could force the wolves into submission; no one would be able to go against his wishes. He was Alpha, but in name only.

He wasn't foolish enough to think that his men had no needs. He knew of their exploits down south to the inns to see the whores. After decades of loneliness, who could blame them? But why steal Sisters? And girls, at that?

"It had to have been bloodsuckers," said Blain. "Our patrols of the forest are the only things standing between the vampires and the humans. We've been doing this for hundreds of years, they were bound to break through at some point. Without the Sisters, our numbers continue to dwindle, even with our exceptionally long life spans."

"No." Adrian shook his head. "Someone has to be helping them. She said that three wolves came into the village. We have to find the culprits and cull them."

"Easy." Blain walked over and set his hands on Adrian's shoulders. "Let's take a second to think about this. If we try to shake down everyone in the pack, the girls will most likely end up dead to cover the trail. We need to feel this out. Do this smart."

Blain's words were wise, but the fact that someone would take the females they were bound to protect was almost more than he could bear. Adrian looked up at his friend. "You should be king."

Blain's brows furrowed, and then he laughed. "Me? No thank you." He held up his hands and crossed to the small nightstand and poured himself a drink.

"You've always been better at diplomacy than I. I'm a react-first-and-think-later person." Adrian swallowed and dropped his gaze to the stone floor. "Too much like my mother that way."

"Don't."

Adrian met Blain's stern gaze,

"Don't you do that. You make your own way in life. When are you going to learn that?"

Adrian shook his head. "Who'd do this, and why?"

"We'll figure it out. But I don't think doing it in the middle of the night is going to help. Together we will stop this from happening again. We'll make sure they are safe."

Adrian blew out a long sigh and sat down on the bed. "You're right."

"Of course I am." Blain smiled, then set down his glass and walked to Adrian, setting his hands on Adrian's shoulders. "You obviously have a lot on your mind right now. You need some sleep. Go to your room–"

"She's in there."

"Is that a problem?"

Adrian lifted his gaze. Blain had a wicked grin on his face. He watched Adrian's reaction, and then laughed heartily. "Well, well, well. Has someone finally tamed your Alpha heart?"

No! "I can't get her out of my thoughts. Her scent is..."

"Is what?"

"Well, you smelled her."

Blain shrugged and moved back to the nightstand. "She smelled like any other woman to me."

Her golden eyes flashed into his mind. The defiant way she'd looked at him when he tried to help her. The distrust he saw when he touched her. "I can't put my finger on it."

Blain smiled. "Pack members tell me that that's how it is with their mates. Her scent is irresistible to them. Sends them into a frenzy, making them want to bed her night and day."

"I know the feeling."

"Then maybe she is the one." Blain had his serious face on again for the second time in a day. That wasn't like him. "Maybe she's the one who will fulfill the prophecy and begin the healing of our lands."

"No." Adrian shook his head. "I have no interest in her more than her safety, and possibly having her find a home here with one of my men." Or me.

"Then stay here tonight." Blain downed his drink. "All that you want her to find needs to wait until she's good and rested. Women don't appreciate being made happy when they are injured. Besides my bed's big enough."

"Fine." Adrian stripped off his shirt. "But don't hog all the covers."

Blain put on an expression of mock sadness. "Thou offendeth me to the core, Sire."

CHAPTER SIX

Redlynn waited for Adrian to return. The pain of her neck and arm overwhelmed her, and no matter what she did, she was unable to get comfortable. After an hour, she simply lay staring at the fire.

She'd never met a man like Adrian. Obviously he was a man of money, but he neither flaunted it, nor bragged about it. He didn't seem to be doing anything with his life. What kind of man did what he wanted, when he wanted? Yet, he had a healer, which meant that there had to be more than just him in the house. Her news of the missing girls had upset him greatly. What she didn't know was why. They weren't from his area. The fact that he didn't seem to fear the beasts perplexed her. There were so many questions. That she'd never heard there were even people living in the forest was just the beginning.

She'd never been outside of Volkzene or the forest. It had been indoctrinated to all of them growing up that Volkzene was home. Outside was nothing but death. Redlynn had never questioned that before now.

Near dawn, Redlynn's eyelids drooped. The sun filtered in through a stained glass window in the corner. She'd never slept in a bed this nice. For as comfortable as it was, the unfamiliarity made her unable to fully relax. Finally, she drifted off to a restless sleep.

She awoke sometime later to the door opening, but she couldn't see it.

She reached under her pillow and grabbed the knife. "Adrian?" she called. She'd been lying in the same position so long that her body was stiff.

The curtain parted at the end of the bed, and a tall, well-built male with blond hair and a handsome angular face stood before her. He was in a dark blue silk tunic and brown breeches. Redlynn clutched the covers around herself. His deep blue eyes watched her, searching for something.

"Hello." He smiled. "Can I help you sit up?"

"Where's Adrian?" She thrust the knife in front of her and pulled her covers up.

"Whoa, easy." He raised his hand in surrender. "I'm not going to hurt you."

"Get out!"

"Hey, take it easy. I just came to see if you were okay. Adrian will be up in a minute. Your eyes—" He stared at her, transfixed.

Redlynn clutched the covers. She could call for help, but who knew what would happen. Had she been brought here just to become the mockery of those in this house, too? Her hand shook from holding out the knife. "Who are you?" she asked forcefully.

"Blain. Sorry," he apologized. "It's just your eyes are so—"

"Cursed?"

"Beautiful."

Redlynn stopped breathing. People were normally scared of her eyes. She and Blain stared at each other for a long while, neither speaking. His face was genuine, but she didn't know him, and a man had never been in her bedroom before. If he tried to attack her, with how she felt, she wasn't sure she'd be able to fend him off too much. She glanced behind him, looking for her things.

"Is it true that you've had girls go missing from your village?"

Redlynn's eyes snapped back to his face. "What do you want?"

"Forgive me." He smiled. It was a nice jovial smile. "I'm Blain. I was with Adrian when we found you. We weren't sure you were going to survive the night."

"That tends to happen when you get attacked by Weres." Redlynn lowered the knife and tried to sit up again, while retaining her modesty.

"The wolves attacked you?"

"Why do you sound amused?" she shot back. "They're wild, cave-dwelling beasts that prey on the blood of the innocent. They have no conscience or remorse, having been cursed by the gods for their blood-thirsty ways."

"You sound like an old mage book," he laughed.

Redlynn's eyes narrowed. She didn't like feeling the fool. "Did you need something?" Her side ached from lying on it too long, and the smugness of Blain was not something she wanted to be dealing with.

"Let me help you."

Before she protested, he wrapped his arm around her waist and helped her into a sitting position. Redlynn's breath caught in her throat at the feel of his hard, hot body. His sapphire blue gaze bore into her. Redlynn held very still at his closeness, making sure her cloak remained closed. The knife protruded toward him. He glanced down at it, and a slight smile played on his face.

"What the hell are you doing?" came a voice from behind Blain.

Blain released her. Adrian burst over to where she now sat, propped against the pillows, and pushed him away.

"Easy." Blain stepped back. "I was helping her sit up. She was in pain, brother."

Adrian held Blain's gaze for a moment before his body relaxed, and he apologized.

"Don't mention it." Blain leaned back against the stone wall.

Redlynn looked from one man to the other; they'd obviously been together for a long while. She wondered if they were brothers by blood.

Adrian turned and sat on the edge of the bed next to her. He lifted his hand as if to touch her, and then ran it through his hair. "Are you okay?"

Something about having him near soothed her. She felt safe with him, a sensation she was not used to. She concealed the knife again.

Adrian sighed. "I told you that you'd be safe here."

"And yet, a man came into this room just moments ago and put his hands on me."

Adrian's brows furrowed and his eyes darkened. He turned his gaze on Blain.

"What?" Blain shrugged. "I was just helping her."

Adrian turned his attention back to her. His face was a hard mask. "Hanna's here to check your wound and to help you bathe. I have a tub in the other room. When she's done examining you, I'll carry you in."

Redlynn's mind fogged over at the nearness of him. Hanna stood with her bag, bow and sword. Her mind snapped into action. She had a job to do. "And then I can leave?"

"Let's see how you're doing first."

Redlynn's eyes narrowed. "You can't keep me here."

Adrian smiled slightly. "I'm sure that is true. But I'm trying to keep you alive. Try to remember that."

The sight of his upturned lips made Redlynn's heart flutter. *Wake up girl!* Why did this man make her feel like a thirteen-year-old girl when she was near him? Something about his presence made her unable to think rationally. She couldn't allow that. She needed to heal and to get back out there. She'd made a promise to her mother and to Anya. She intended on fulfilling it.

Adrian walked to where Blain stood against the wall, watching her. He punched Blain in the shoulder and Blain broke eye contact with her, smiling at Adrian and backing away.

"What? I just wanted to meet her," he said under his breath. "I wasn't doing anything."

"Get out," Adrian growled, pushing Blain toward the door.

Blain laughed heartily and whispered something to Adrian that Redlynn couldn't hear. A growl escaped Adrian, and Blain's smile widened.

"My Lady, I doth apologize. Both for intrudeth-ing upon thee, and for putteth-ing my hands upon thy person." Then he gave a flourishing bow.

Adrian grabbed Blain by the arm, raising him from his bow, and escorted him to the door.

Blain smiled at Redlynn. "Feel better, golden sister. I want to see you wield that big sword." He waved, and then was gone.

Adrian scowled and motioned to Hanna, who'd been sitting quietly at the table, waiting.

The woman had soft features, delicate and fine. Several small wrinkles creased her brown eyes, but not enough that Redlynn would consider her old. Forty was Redlynn's guess. Hanna had light brown hair pulled into a long braid.

"Have we met?" Redlynn studied the woman's face.

"Perhaps." Hanna smiled. "I didn't always live here. Where are you from?"

"Volkzene."

"Ahhhh... home of the Sisterhood of Red."

"My name is Redlynn."

"May I check your wound this morning?"

"I checked it a few hours ago. You did well with the salve. However, there isn't much to see, with the fernblend and all."

Hanna chuckled and then whispered, "M'lord meant well, dear."

60

Redlynn glanced up to Adrian's face. A look of pure annoyance was planted there. She smiled to herself. He was strikingly handsome when he scowled. His face softened at her smile and Redlynn felt her cheeks flame. She looked away.

Hanna leaned in, pulled up the sheet to cover Redlynn's chest, and removed the bandage on her neck and shoulder. Taking a damp cloth, she wiped at the salve and leaves. Redlynn winced at the pain, but was surprised that the leaves wiped away easily. Hanna's brows furrowed. Redlynn glanced at her shoulder. The skin was red and raw and new, but no wound remained. There was no way she should have healed that quickly.

"What was in your salve?"

"Comfrey, calendula, plantain, eucalyptus. But it's never done that before."

"Maybe it was the fernblend," Adrian added.

"I doubt that," Hanna mused.

"Must be." He gave a triumphant grin.

Redlynn and Hanna didn't respond. Hanna checked Redlynn's shoulder and then her collarbone. It was her shoulder that pained the most.

"It's dislocated," Hanna said. "We have to set it. But with your collarbone broken, putting it in is really going to hurt. Unfortunately, we can't wait, or your shoulder will heal wrong." Hanna looked at Redlynn quizzically.

"What?"

"You should be in unbearable agony right now." Hanna shook her head.

Redlynn gave a half shrug. "I've always had a high tolerance for pain."

Hanna glanced over at Adrian and then back to Redlynn.

"Do you know how to set it?" Redlynn asked.

"No."

"I do," said Adrian. His smile had been wiped away. "Bathe her first. It will help her relax. Then I'll do it." He walked to the door. "I'll check to see if the water is ready."

After he left, Redlynn asked, "Why do you call him 'my Lord?'"

"Because this is his castle."

"Castle?" Redlynn had to admit that the Sisterhood knew very little about what lay in the woods that they guarded against. But she'd never, ever heard of people living in Wolvenglen before now. "Why do you live out here? Aren't you scared of the Weres?"

"No. I'm not scared of the wolves. There are a great many other things in this wood, and in this world, that I am more afraid of, Red."

Redlynn studied Hanna's face again. "My mother used to call me Red. She was a good woman. She always tried to make me feel special, because of my eyes."

"You are special," Hanna said.

"Were-eyes. That's what people whispered."

Hanna's presence made Redlynn speak words she'd never told another. The sensation surprised her. She'd been more welcomed and attended to with kindness since coming to Wolvenglen than she had in her twenty-four years of life in Volkzene. Her heart surged. Maybe they'd let her return and stay after she killed the Weres. Redlynn pushed the thought away quickly. *Don't be silly.* She shouldn't presume they wanted anything more than to heal her and send her on her way. But Adrian...

"Your eyes are beautiful. My Lord thinks so."

Redlynn raised her brows. "He told you that?"

"No. But he spoke to Blain before we came up. And he trusts Blain like no other, so if he told Blain that, then it must be true."

"No man has ever thought of me as beautiful before."

"That's because what most men want is a submissive little wife who will cook and have babies," Hanna laughed.

"Is that what your husband expects of you?"

"Oh, no. The men of Wolvenglen aren't like other men. They like their women strong and fiery."

"My mother used to be a midwife and healer in Volkzene."

"Did she?" asked Hanna, smoothing the covers.

"Yes. I suppose they'd hoped I'd take her place when she died." Redlynn opened her mouth to ask something, but Adrian returned. He moved over to the bed and closed the curtains, then ordered several people to enter. Moments later, water splashed into a tub.

When everyone had left, he opened the curtains. "Let me carry you to the bath."

"I'm just fine." Redlynn grabbed her cloak and swung her legs over the side of the bed. She swayed slightly and Hanna grabbed her by the elbow, steadying her.

"Obviously, you're not." Adrian rounded the bed.

"I said, I'm fine." Adrian put his hand out to help her, but she shoved him away. "I can do it."

He pursed his lips and crossed his arms over his chest. He huffed once, and then said, "Okay then, after you." He waved her toward the bathing room.

She didn't move. He was treating her like a child and she didn't care for it. "I can bathe myself as well. I've been doing it for a few years now."

Adrian inclined his head.

Each step sapped Redlynn of her strength, but she refused to let it show. Her body felt like a rope twisted too tight. Each movement stiff and painful. Slower than she wanted to, she made her way to the bathroom. Stepping up and through the threshold, steam from the water moistened her face. It'd been a long time since she'd felt a hot bath. And she'd never seen a tub in a room of its own before. Breathing in the perfumed water, she relaxed.

Redlynn turned to find Adrian watching. Hanna slid into the room behind her, and closed the heavy door.

"Let me help you out of your clothes, dear."

Redlynn opened her mouth, but Hanna raised her hand.

"Stop right there. You want to be brave for Adrian, wonderful, but not with me. You're hurting, and you have nothing to prove to me. I already know how strong you are. Let me help you."

I like her.

Without waiting for an answer, Hanna undressed Redlynn and eased her into the tub. She couldn't hold in the sigh that escaped her lips at the warmth of the water.

Hanna reached into her pouch, pulled out a canister, stepped up to the tub and knelt on the floor. "Let me help cleanse the area of the bite."

Redlynn nodded and leaned to the right. The stretching of her neck pained her shoulder and collarbone. Redlynn winced and bit her lip.

Hanna hummed, gently working the soap into the wound. The tune was familiar but Redlynn couldn't place it. "What is that you are humming?"

"An old lullaby my mother used to sing to me. Do you have a family, Red?"

Redlynn swallowed hard. "Not anymore. My father was driven off by a Were when I was young. It broke my mother's heart. She missed my father every day. She died a few years ago, and the only other person I called family died two nights ago. Killed by the Weres that I was in the process of eradicating when I was brought here."

"How do you know it was Weres?" Hanna asked.

"The Head of my Order confirmed seeing them."

"Hmmm…" Hanna mused, rubbing the soap down Redlynn's arms.

"What?"

"Oh, it's probably nothing, but I was just thinking. How would wolves grab a girl and carry her away?"

Redlynn's mind raced. It'd always been the Weres that'd taken the girls, or so they'd been told. But Hanna was right, how'd Weres get the girls out?

A knock pulled her from her thoughts. "Is everything okay in there?"

"We're fine," Hanna called. "But we need some towels."

"Of course," said Adrian.

Hanna looked at Redlynn and smiled. "He's a good man. He's tough, and scared to let anyone in, but a good man."

"You know him well?"

Hannah nodded. "We all know each other well enough here. But, they're all good men." Hanna stood and put the soap away.

"All?"

"Yes, most of his subjects are men. There are about fifty of them here right now."

"No women?"

"There are a few of us here. But let's be honest," Hanna laughed. "The forest isn't the kind of place most women want to live in."

It was true. Redlynn loved the woods. She always had. But she couldn't imagine many people did. "Why don't the men leave?"

"This is their home. They know nothing else."

There was another knock. Hanna slid the door open slightly and Adrian passed the towels through the gap to her. Hanna held up the towel like a shield and averted her eyes. Redlynn grasped the right side of the tub with her good hand and got her feet underneath herself. She tried to stand but the tub was slick with soapy water and she slipped, crying out.

"I can't get up," she grunted.

"Here, let me help." Hanna dropped the towel and wrapped her arm around Redlynn's waist. She tried to lift Redlynn, but Redlynn cried out again.

This time the knock was loud. "What's going on?"

"I can't take her out," Hanna called.

The door swung inward and Adrian stood at Redlynn's back. She hunched over, letting her hair cover her body. Adrian bent down into the water to draw her up, but she pushed him away. Her body flushed with heat.

"I'm naked."

He took a deep breath and turned away. "I'll close my eyes."

"You can still feel me, can't you?"

Redlynn let out an indignant 'Hey,' as he bent down a second time and lifted her.

She protested and slipped in his grip.

"Don't do that, or we'll both go down," he commanded.

Redlynn swallowed and put her good arm around his neck for support. Their eyes met and she licked her lips involuntarily. His hard muscles flexed around her and her thighs warmed, even though the air chilled her skin. Walking out of the bathing room, Adrian sat her on the end of the bed and turned away.

"Get her in a gown, and then I'll set her shoulder," he said in a gruff voice.

Hanna returned with the nightgown and lifted the soft cotton over Redlynn before maneuvering it over her arm and shoulder. She winced, but refused to cry out yet again. The soft material fell down to her ankles. The cocoon of the gown comforted her. *Why does everything here feel so nice?* Redlynn took a deep breath. She couldn't afford to get used to it; soon she'd be leaving.

CHAPTER SEVEN

Adrian listened as Redlynn dressed. The heat from the fire was nothing compared to how his imagination was heating him. The glimpse of her breast the night before was more than enough to get his blood pumping. And now that he'd felt her skin on his, his mind conjured images of what it'd be like to have her soft skin beneath him as— Stop! He was acting like a lovesick pup. He couldn't let this happen. He needed to get out and run off his tension. That, and he needed to get her out of his bed.

"She's ready," said Hanna.

He coughed, pulled from his thoughts. He rolled his shoulders and turned. Her thick, red hair hung to her hips, and her skin had regained a bit of its peachy glow. She was impossibly more beautiful without the dirt and blood smears on her angelic face. Get her shoulder set, and get her into her own bed, that was the plan.

"Hanna, move to the other side, please. Put your arms around her waist and hold her." Adrian surveyed Redlynn, trying to find the best angle. He was going to have to touch her. There was no way around it.

Hanna obeyed.

"Alright." Adrian sat on the bed trying not to stare into her beautiful golden eyes. "This is going to hurt."

"I assumed it would."

Strong and stubborn. He admired her strength, but having been through dislocations before, nothing could prepare her for the pain that was coming. "I'm going to get your arm in position first."

Redlynn took a deep breath and nodded.

He took a deep breath himself. He could do this. He reached up and grasped her wrist lightly; his heartbeat quickened, and his wolf snarled. "Make a fist." Moving her elbow in toward her body, he formed a right angle, and then moved her hand close to her stomach. "I'm going to rotate your arm outward, slowly. Do you need something to bite down on?"

Redlynn shook her head. She took a deep breath, but her eyes betrayed her fear. Hanna wrapped her arms around Redlynn's waist and leaned backward to add counterweight. Her skin held the faint scent of herbs, and her hands were calloused from years of using a bow.

Focus, he needed to focus. Adrian pulled out on Redlynn's wrist, while making sure her elbow stayed by her side. The grimace on her face told him the pain was building. She shut her eyes tight and as he moved her wrist out further. She whimpered. His grip faltered, he wanted to stop, but couldn't. When he had the wrist almost parallel to her body, Redlynn screamed.

"Hold her!" Adrian yelled at Hanna.

"Stop! Stop!" Redlynn cried.

"Just a little more." Seeing her in such pain made him wish he could rip his own heart out for hurting her.

Redlynn screamed again and Adrian let go. She pulled her arm instinctively to her side, cradling it. Tears streamed down her cheeks, but she made no sound except for her labored breaths. A ripple skimmed over him and he had to get up and stretch, trying to keep his wolf at bay. Several sets of footsteps rushed down the hall. Adrian turned. Blain, Dax and Hanna's husband, Fendrick, burst in. Fendrick's wild eyes scanned the room. He rushed to the bed and gathered Hanna into his arms.

"Are you alright, my darling? I heard screaming."

"No, no, Sweeting." She stroked his cheek. "It's Red. Her arm's dislocated."

Fendrick looked over at Redlynn and then at Adrian. "I apologize, M'lord, for bursting into your private rooms."

Adrian continued to stretch. "No offense taken. It is completely understandable."

"Can she leave now?" Fendrick scanned Hanna once more.

"The arm is still out. I need to try again," Hanna said.

"I'll help." Blain stepped closer and locked eyes on Adrian. "Let Fendrick and Hanna leave."

Adrian didn't want another male anywhere near Redlynn, but Hanna kept Fendrick stable. They were all lucky he'd only burst into the room. Adrian often wondered why Hanna had chosen Fendrick of all of his eligible men. But it was good for all of them that she had.

He nodded. "Go, Hanna."

Hanna glanced at Redlynn. "I'll check on you."

"Is there anything I can do?" asked Dax.

Adrian tried to concentrate. The room seemed unusually warm. "Get her some whisky for the pain." He walked to the window and opened it, letting the cool breeze rush over his skin, calming him.

"Give her this." Hanna reached into her bag, pulling out a bottle.

"What is it?" Redlynn croaked.

"Opia."

Redlynn laughed. "And you are only now offering it to me?"

"It is hard to come by, and the addiction factor is very high."

"Give the girl a dropper full," Blain said. "She's earned it from what it sounded like out there."

"Come, darling." Fendrick pulled on Hanna. Dax followed them out.

"Blain, you do it." Blain gave Adrian a quizzical look, and then took the bottle from Hanna, filled the dropper, and placed it on Redlynn's tongue. She winced, but swallowed. She relaxed almost immediately and her eyes glazed a bit. Sadly, her skin regained the waxy sheen from the night before, and a fine layer of sweat covered her body. Adrian watched her from across the room. The bitter scent of pain wafted off of her.

"I'll pull, you hold." Blain moved next to her.

Redlynn's eyes met his, pleading. His chest squeezed.

"It'll be okay. Blain's better than I at this." Adrian crossed to the bed, taking a deep breath. He could do this. His arms shook as her pulled her tight into his chest. Her cool skin felt good through his shirt. Her hair fell over his arms as he wrapped them around her, the scent reaching into him and making his head fuzzy. He wasn't attracted to her. He had no interest in finding a mate.

"Hey, Princess."

"I'm not a princess," Redlynn slurred.

"Oh, sorry, huntress then." Blain laughed. "I'm going to do this in one shot, alright?"

"Just get on with it." She gritted her teeth.

"Easy," Adrian soothed. His gaze met Blain's. "Let's go." He hoped Blain made quick work of it.

Blain nodded, grasped her wrist, locked eyes with Adrian, and began to turn her shoulder out once more. Her body quaked and Adrian tightened his grip. Blain had her arm almost totally extended before she cried out. His wolf snapped and snarled as she screamed, begging them to stop. Adrian held her closer and murmured comforting words into her hair, as much for himself as for her. The ripples started in Adrian's gut and spread through him like wildfire. He was close to shifting.

Blain had been with Adrian long enough to see the signs. He knew what was coming. There was a quick jerk and a pop.

70

Redlynn screamed and then cut off. Pulling her arm close, she curled into Adrian's chest.

He wrapped his arms around her protectively and lay back on the pillows. Her breath burst from her chest. After several minutes, she sighed and relaxed. He was far from relaxed, however. He'd fought the shift, his heart beating wildly in his chest. Adrenaline coursed through him, leaving him needing an outlet.

"I'll leave you two alone." Blain moved to the door.

"Remind me to return the favor sometime," Redlynn said.

"I hope not," he laughed.

Blain left with a silent close of the doors. Adrian reveled in the feel of Redlynn in his arms. It felt so natural for her to be there. It had been too long since he'd felt the touch of a woman. She looked up at him and licked her lips. Adrian's heartbeat quickened. He told himself that he needed to get her into her own room. But his body didn't move.

"That, I think, was the worst pain I've ever felt," she said.

"You think?"

"Pain's always been part of my life, one way or another. The emotional pain lessened when I was nine, to some degree."

"Pain is something I am very familiar with; on a daily basis, sometimes." The wolf change was nothing short of excruciating. "For someone who had a dislocated shoulder, you didn't show signs of distress till the end."

"Until you started pulling on my arm the pain was something I could handle. Broken bones, cuts, bruises, something called a concussion. You say it, I've probably had it. I even had a dislocated finger once. My mother always said I had a high threshold for pain."

"Why so many injuries?"

"I was always trying to prove myself to the Sisterhood, my father, myself. I pushed myself harder and further every day."

He stared down at her flushed cheeks and ran a finger down one side of her face. "What happened when you were nine?"

"That's how old I was when I got the concussion. My father left us soon after. He was… a hard man."

She stared off as if remembering.

Adrian's gut clenched and his wolf snapped in anger. "He beat you."

She looked up. "No. My mother wouldn't have stood for that. He had other ways of making us feel like nothing though. He drank and talked. He liked to talk. My mother took the brunt of it. But I was the object of his wrath nonetheless. I can't remember him ever saying even a kind word to me." She stared off again, her eyes glassy from the opia. "It was my red hair and strange eyes. When I was nine her went into a drunken rage, it was nothing new, but this time he lashed out. I don't really think he meant to strike me, but my mother didn't give him a second chance. She sent me out of the hut for the evening. He was gone before I returned."

The anger inside Adrian bloomed into a heating inferno. "A male abusing his mate and child."

"You sound surprised. Surely you've seen it here in Wolvenglen."

Adrian's gaze hardened. "No," he said firmly. "Females are sacred here. If one of my men hit his mate or child he would be cast out of Wolvenglen forever. If not worse."

"Cast out?" She shook her head. "Wolvenglen is quite different from Volkzene. There everyone turned a blind eye to my mother's plight. No one asked, no one helped."

He stared at her, silent for a minute. "Humanity truly has fallen far in Volkzene. Even though it pains me to stay here, without my mother and father, I am glad I live in Wolvenglen."

"You miss them. Your parents."

"Do you miss your mother?"

She swallowed. "Every day."

72

"So it is with me. Like your father, my mother left when I was only fift—teen," he finished.

"But you had your father."

"In a way I guess. He was here in body, but his spirit gave up after my mother disappeared. He shut everyone out, including me."

His gaze travelled to the portrait of his mother and father above the fireplace.

"I would have loved growing up all the way out here. One of the things that used to anger my father the most was that my mother would bring me into the forest to gather herbs and roots and berries. I always felt at home amongst the trees and animals and the sungolds. We don't have yellow flowers like sungolds in Volkzene. Only Wolfsbane is permitted. My mother used to let me pick them to bring home."

"That's how I feel running through Wolvenglen. The rush of wind on my face, the dew on my tongue. A handful of draepon berries to suck on. It's where I'm truly happy."

"When I was sick my mother used to lay me in the riverbed and let the cool water flow over me. Then she would lay me on the moss and we'd stare up at the stars till the fever passed. I used to think that one day I would be queen of the wood and I'd live in it forever."

She glanced at him quickly and then looked away.

"You're embarrassed?"

She looked at him again. "I've never told anyone that. It's all stupid girlish fantasies."

"Every girl should have fantasies."

"Not where I come from. Not in my father's house."

"But you said you're father is gone."

"Some lessons stick with you, no matter how far away the teacher goes." She shrugged her good shoulder. "It doesn't matter, that all changed for me anyway."

"Why?"

"My mother died. It wasn't the same without her. For a while I would still come, but not too far in. Then Lillith forbade us and the Were attacks started and it just– It no longer felt like home. I'm not surprised though. I knew it couldn't last forever. I've never fit in anywhere."

He chuckled. "I have a hard time believing that. You must have had men lining up to marry you in Volkzene."

Her brows knit together. "Are you mocking me?"

He dropped his smile. "Why would I mock you?"

"Men have never been interested in me."

"Surely you jest."

"Look at me. I'm stubborn, opinionated, strong. I dress like a man. I don't sew or cook or clean or do any of the things a wife should do."

"Who told you that?" he asked. *Who'd been so cruel as to break her spirit? A fool, that's who.*

"It doesn't matter because he was right."

"He was wrong, and you're wrong for believing him."

Her cheeks flushed and she looked away. He turned her face back.

"Maybe you just haven't met the right man. Cooking and sewing are useful but they don't make a women desirable. Out here we like our women strong and opinionated. If they weren't, nothing would ever get done."

"*Cursed.* That's what they called me. Because of my eyes, they believed I was cursed. 'Were eyes', they said. They thought that any man who married me would be cursed with the same eyes for bedding me. And our children would be the same."

"That's ridiculous. Cursed because of the color of eyes you were born with? What about those with black hair? Or those born without a limb, or dumb or blind? Were they cursed as well? What did you do that was so wrong that the gods cursed you before you even got here?"

74

She held his gaze for a long minute. Her coloring had improved a bit and her eyelids drooped ever so slightly.

"I'm sorry you went through that," he said.

Her gaze hardened. "Don't pity me."

"I don't. It's obviously shaped you into the woman you are and you're stronger for it. I'm just sorry that that is what it took to get you here."

"Into your bed?"

He couldn't speak. Her sweet breath fell lightly on his skin, cooling it.

"Why did you save me in the woods?"

Because you are the most beautiful woman I have ever seen, and probably the one I am meant to take as a mate. "Because you were hurt."

"But you don't know me."

Adrian's eyebrows drew together. "Does that matter?"

"Most people would have left me for dead."

Anger soured his thoughts once more. Is that what had become of the Sisterhood? Were all males outside of Wolvenglen so callous? How could someone not stop and help a female in need? "Well, I'm not most people."

"No. You're not." Her gaze shifted to his lips. She touched his cheek, and then ran her fingers through his long hair. "Your hair's soft."

Adrian didn't dare breathe. A flesh-and-blood woman with golden eyes and the mark of the wolf was in his arms. It went against everything he'd promised himself he wouldn't do. All the other females he'd said no to. All the years spent burying any desire to find a mate and settle down. All the times he told himself he wouldn't end up like his father. Bending his head, he breathed her in. She lifted her chin. Their lips were inches apart and he tasted her breath in his mouth.

"Adrian," she whispered. "Your heart is racing."

75

"Like I said before, whoever told you that you weren't desirable because you can't cook, is a fool."

She licked her bottom lip and before he could stop himself, he plunged down and closed the distance between them. The moan that escaped her was enough to send his wolf howling for more. Tangling his hand in her hair, he guided her mouth to his more fully. Her lips parted and their tongues mingled in a soft swirl. His mind went numb. Adrian pressed closer to her, and her arm twitched. He pulled away quickly.

"Are you alright?" He searched her face for signs of distress.

"It's my shoulder."

Dammit! He shouldn't be doing this. It wasn't fair to lead her on. Especially with her medicated. "You should rest." He laid her on the pillow.

"Yes." Her eyes held desire and resistance. "I'm sorry for taking your bed again."

Me, too. "It's fine. I can stay somewhere else."

"You can stay."

Adrian swallowed. It had gone too far. She wanted him to stay. Part of him wanted to say yes.

"I should go. I have things that need to be attended to." Adrian's wolf was close to the surface. His Alpha male sat up and begged like a mutt.

Her eyes closed and he turned to leave. He glanced back at her. A ray of sunlight from the window streamed across her face. He fought the urge to feel her in his arms again. He had to get out of there before he did something he'd regret.

CHAPTER EIGHT

When Redlynn awoke, the lamps had been lit and the sky was dark outside the window. The effects of the Opia had dissipated, but left her groggy and not quite herself. An uncomfortable ache in her belly and a tightness between her thighs bothered her. She wondered if she was close to getting her women's time. Groaning at the thought, she rolled over. The other side of the bed was empty.

The memory of kissing Adrian assaulted her. What the heck had happened? One minute he'd been holding her as unbearable pain shot through her, the next she had his warm lips on hers. His lips had been full and soft and his tongue had danced warmly with hers, making her entire body tingle with anticipation. As the memory flooded back, the same tingle shot through her limbs and pooled between her thighs. She'd never been kissed before.

Wake up! You have a job to do. She rolled her shoulders to find the pain had eased.

It was unexplainable. It didn't make any sense that she felt this way for a man she hadn't known for more than two days. The women in her village courted for months before settling down. She wondered if this was how it had been with their men from the very beginning. Redlynn grasped her locket through her gown and wished that her mother were around to talk to. Or even Anya.

A howl broke through her thoughts. She sat up quickly. She should be out there tracking them down, not lying in bed like a birthing sow. Redlynn got to her feet and moved quickly toward the table where her things lay. A wave of nausea hit her. The mix of Opia and lack of food in her stomach had her reeling, but it didn't matter. She dragged herself to the table. Her pack was exactly as she'd left it. Her sword and bow lay waiting as well. *Crap!* She couldn't shoot. Not with her arm out of commission.

Her arm hadn't been rewrapped to her side. Redlynn rotated and slowly extending it. Her arm shook, but held. She picked up her bow and tested the weight. Her left hand gripped the shaft. Grabbing an arrow from her quiver, she notched it in place, took a deep breath and steadied her left arm. With her right hand, she pulled the bow string taut. Her collarbone screamed in pain, and her shoulder tremored. Her aim would never be true. If she went out there now, she'd be lucky to hit a sleeping dragon.

"What are you doing?"

She spun and lost her grip. The arrow flew toward the door. Blain reached out and caught it.

Redlynn scowled. "What does it look like?" She set the bow down.

"Like you want me to shove your shoulder into place again."

"I'm—"

"Fine." Blain nodded. "Yes, I've heard you keep telling people that."

Redlynn turned away from his smirk and fiddled with her things. He was so infuriating. She'd never met a man who teased her the way he did. His arrogance and laissez faire attitude were in stark contrast to Adrian's solemn demeanor. She'd seen men like him in the village. She'd always felt sorry for the Sisters who married them. "Can I help you with something?"

"I just came to check on you. See if you're hungry."

She watched out of the corner of her eye as he walked up to where she stood, inspecting the arrow he'd caught.

"Not a bad arrow," he said. "Quite good, actually. A little on the large side though."

"I want to make sure that what I hit, I kill." She grabbed the arrow from his prying fingers and placed it in her quiver.

"I bet." Blain's gaze drifted down over her form.

Looking down, she noticed how thin her gown was. Embarrassed, she crossed her arms in front of her breasts.

"Sorry." Blain turned away with a laugh. "We don't have too many females out our way."

Redlynn got the distinct impression that he used laughter to hide his insecurities.

"With men staring at them all the time, I can see why not."

"Ouch." Blain laughed and covered his heart with his hands. "Thou dost wound me to the core, M'lady."

Redlynn shook her head and blew out a heavy breath. She didn't have time for such nonsense. "Where's Adrian? I need to get going."

"He went out for the evening."

"Because of the Weres? The howl awakened me."

"So, are you hungry then?"

He was avoiding her question. But she needed strength, and food might help quash the nausea, and the cramping. "I could eat, but then I need to go. I told Adrian–"

"Good." He smiled. "I'll bring us some food. There are clothes in the bathroom if you wish to put something on."

Interesting how he speaks to me, but ignores what I say. Blain's casual nature and seeming familiarity with her struck Redlynn as odd. She realized that if she'd ever had a brother, he might treat her the way Blain did. Growing up, people had never been so friendly with her. But everyone she'd seen or met in Wolvenglen had been like... *family.* It was weird, but she'd been more at ease here than she ever had with her mother in Volkzene. It was crazy. She had no reason to be comfortable or safe here; she barely knew these people.

Conflict built within her. The Weres were still out there, and they needed to be stopped. The Were King needed to be killed as retribution for what he'd done to Anya and her father. Her heartbeat quickened at the thought that she might have a chance at happiness in Wolvenglen. If she ran off now– She'd been banished. She had nowhere else.

Redlynn shook her head, trying to clear it. *It's the Opia making me weak-minded. Confusing me and lowering my defenses. I have a job to do.* She'd give it one more day of healing, and no more. She swallowed the dryness in her throat. No matter how right it felt being here in the woods, she had to finish what she came to do. Maybe after... if she lived through it... maybe then... Don't be silly! The people of the castle had kept peace with the Weres for years. If she went after them, she doubted she'd be welcomed back with open arms. A thought struck her. What if she weren't successful and the Weres took out their retribution on the very people who'd taken her in? Redlynn straightened her back. She'd just have to succeed, then.

She stepped away from the table, and Blain and walked through the doorway of the bathing room. She closed the door and turned to find the clothes. She groaned. *A dress.* She wasn't wearing that.

A deep red, silk gown with golden brocaded sungolds at the hem hung in the window. Next to it sat a vase of matching sungolds. The gesture touched her that he'd remembered her saying they were her favorite, but Redlynn hadn't worn a dress since she was twelve. The dress was beautiful, she had to admit, and again it was strange to see such finery in the woods.

"I can't wear this," she called.

"If it's the wrong color, there's a whole closet full in the next room. I can bring you a different one."

"No. It isn't the color it's… a dress."

Blain roared with laughter and Redlynn cursed under her breath. "I told Adrian you wouldn't wear it. Bet him five silver you wouldn't even try it on. But he picked it out himself."

Something inside her wanted to please Adrian by wearing it. But a bigger part of her didn't want Blain to win the bet.

Before she changed her mind, she lifted her nightgown off and threw it to the ground. She strode naked to the washbasin, poured water into it and used a towel to wipe her face and breasts. Then she ran the towel under her armpits and between her legs. When she finished she used the chamber pot and shivered naked, staring at the gown.

"You alright in there? Need some help?" Blain teased.

"I'm–" Redlynn blew out an angry breath. *I'm fine!* "I'll be out in a minute."

Redlynn took the cloth between her fingers. She'd never worn anything of such great quality before. Her mother hadn't been able to afford anything more than the occasional cotton frock. Inadequacy rushed over her.

Oh, what the hell? With great care, Redlynn worked the dress onto her body. She was used to seeing herself in her shapeless tunics and breeches. She was surprised to see how much a dress accentuated her womanliness. Her breasts were too exposed and the dress hugged her waist. The only problem was her birthmark. In the low cut of the dress, the mark was partially visible. Redlynn tried to cover it with the side of the fabric, but it did no good. Moving her locket clasp behind her neck, she arranged the locket between her breasts.

"You sure you don't need my help?" Blain's voice now more concerned than jovial.

Redlynn took a deep breath and opened the door. Blain sat relaxing in a chair with his boots up on an adjoining chair. He'd just thrown a grape into the air, but when he saw her, it missed his mouth and hit him in the eye, not fazing him. His smile fell as he stared motionless.

"What?" she demanded.

He cleared his throat. "Nothing," he croaked, his eyes dropping to the table. His feet hit the floor and he took a large swig from his goblet. "Come eat." He glanced up at her.

"What?" she demanded again, trying to pull the fabric over her birthmark. "Why are you looking at me so?"

Blain lifted his gaze and shrugged, shoving his mouth full of chicken.

Redlynn sighed exasperatedly and sat next to him. Her plate had been piled high with grapes, cheese, bread and chicken.

She picked up the chicken and bit into it. As soon as it hit her mouth, she found herself ravishingly hungry. The chicken was tender and juicy. Blain silently watched her devour everything on her plate and down several glasses of mead. When she'd finished, she thought her dress was going to pop. Standing she tried to stretch, but her arm had had enough for one day and wailed in protest.

"You know you shouldn't be able to do that."

"Do what?"

"Move that shoulder. It takes weeks to heal. And your throat is barely discolored now, like the wound is months old."

"Maybe it was Hanna's salve," she suggested.

"Maybe. Or maybe it's you."

"What does that mean?" Redlynn snapped. How many times had she been teased for being different? And now Blain was doing it, too?

Blain studied her for another minute, and then smiled, "You want to see what Wolvenglen's like outside of this room?"

82

"Yes." She'd never heard better words in her life. She wanted more than anything to leave the room. What she should be doing is getting out to the woods.

Blain stood from his chair and held out his arm for her. "The wolves will still be there after you rest for a few more days. Besides, you wouldn't want to leave without saying goodbye to Adrian."

She studied Blain. How had he known she was thinking about leaving?

He smiled and held his arm out further for her to hold. "I won't bite."

"But I might." She gave a slight smile.

Blain's laugh boomed through the room. It brought a real smile to her lips. She wasn't the joking type, but somehow Blain's humor was contagious. And he was right. She was dying to explore the castle before she left.

"Come on, golden sister." He took her hand and laid it on his arm. "Bite me if you have to, just don't fall. Adrian would kill me if anything happened to you."

"Oh, I'm sure he will be happy to be rid of me, so he can have his room back."

Blain gave her a sideways glance. "Adrian likes his space, it's true. But I have a feeling you'll be good for him."

"Because I'm so trying?"

"No, because you're special."

"Trust me. I'm not as special as you think. I'm simply a woman who wants to end the suffering of her village once and for all."

"The village that doesn't want you."

Redlynn's eyebrows creased.

"Come on." He showed her out the door.

The hallway was the same grey stone that her room was made of. Lit lanterns hung from the ceiling and a dark rug stretched in both directions. Doors lined the hallway to the left.

"This is Adrian's wing of the castle. Only his room is in use right now."

They walked a short way to the end of the hall, and then turned down an adjoining one. A landing connected to a staircase. Voices and dishes clinking floated from somewhere up ahead.

They rounded a small corner and the wall cut in half. A giant room lay below. Three long, wooden tables, big enough to hold over thirty people at a time, sat perpendicular to a main table. Behind the main table, on the wall, hung a large coat of arms: black with a red bow and arrow over an eye. She found herself overwhelmed by the sight of the dining hall. Two of the tables were close to full of men.

A man noticed her, stopped talking and elbowed the man next to him. Before she knew what was happening, all the men had stopped eating and were staring at her.

Under the scrutinizing gaze of the men, her skin flushed with heat. There were so many of them; all large, handsome and strong.

"Why are they looking at me like that?" Her eyes narrowed and she glanced at Blain. A chill ran up her spine and her cheeks felt flush.

"Because you're stunning," Blain whispered into her hair.

The men continued to watch her.

"Make them stop." Redlynn pressed her lips together.

Blain laughed. "This is Redlynn," he called. "She is Lord Adrian's guest."

In unison, all the men stood and bowed to her. Redlynn cleared her throat, but said nothing. As the men stood, watching her, a bustle of women and children came in through a door in the corner. Upon seeing the men all on their feet, they stopped. Spotting her, each woman curtsied to Redlynn in turn. The children, boys and girls from young to early teen, waved to her, as well. Hanna held a baby and had two children hanging onto her dress.

"Well, go ahead and eat." Blain waved his hand at the group. "We're going for a walk."

Everyone took their seats again, but the men who didn't have a spouse continued to watch her as she proceeded down the stairs. When she reached the bottom, Hanna walked over to meet them.

"Hello, Red. You seem to be doing well." Hanna exchanged a look with Blain that Redlynn couldn't read.

"It is nice to be up and about." Redlynn peeked around her at the men. Why were they still staring? It couldn't be her eyes. They couldn't even see them from that distance. She wanted to drop her gaze, but refused. Looking at the men she narrowed her gaze. They were rugged and handsome. Large and muscular. Not like the farmers of Volkzene.

"How's your shoulder?" Hanna asked.

"Sore." Redlynn continued to stare until the men finally looked away and went back to their food. All except for three. Two dark-haired males that looked similar, and an older rugged male with red hair and a red beard.

"To be expected. I'm going to eat with Fendrick, and then I'll come to see you."

"You don't need to do that." Redlynn met Hanna's eye. "I'm feeling much better and I'll be leaving soon."

"No. I want to. I'll be up in a little bit," Hanna smiled and squeezed Redlynn's arm lightly.

Hanna's smile untied the knots in Redlynn's stomach. She gave Hanna a tight smile and nodded.

"Come on, golden sister." Blain patted her arm.

Hanna moved away and Blain showed Redlynn to the other end of the feasting hall. An enormous fireplace took up half a wall. As they neared it, she broke into a light sweat. Above hung an enormous ornate mirror. The frame swirled with flowers and birds. At the very top sat a red rose made from a large red stone. It was truly a work of art.

"That's beautiful," Redlynn mused.

"It's been in Adrian's family for generations." He pointed to the corner where the women had entered from. "Down there is the kitchen."

"Do the women do all the cooking?"

"They do most of it. But we've all learned to cook over the years, as well."

That was definitely different than in Volkzene.

"Over there." He pointed to another door. "Leads to where the rest of the men and women stay."

"They don't have their own homes?"

"We tend to be a close-knit group here in Wolvenglen. But we have more than enough rooms. As a matter of fact, many are empty at the moment."

"Where do you go for privacy?"

"The forest." Blain pushed open the outer door and they walked into a foyer. "This is the entrance hall." He let go of her and gestured to the long line of large portraits hanging on the right and left of the hall. "These paintings have been done of all of our rulers since we settled here."

Redlynn stood in awe. There were dozens of paintings. Studying them in turn, she noticed each bore a similar likeness. The men were broad-shouldered and strong, the women stately and beautiful.

For several minutes, Blain pointed to a few, telling her about the rich history of the people in the paintings. The women reminded Redlynn of what she imagined her ancestors, the Heads of the Order, would've looked like. She noticed a light spot on the wall with a missing painting. Next to it, the last painting, was that of a lone man.

"That's Adrian." Redlynn stopped in front of it.

"Actually, it's his father."

"Where is he?" She studied the face that was so similar to Adrian's. Even the sadness that seemed to radiate off of the image reminded her of him.

"Adrian's father betrayed his mother, and she fled. He died of a broken heart."

"What did he do?"

"He was tricked into lying with another."

Redlynn snorted. "Tricked? How can a man be tricked into sleeping with someone else?"

Blain sighed. "He was seduced by magick. But the queen didn't see it that way. All she saw was that he'd broken their wedding vow. She refused to forgive and instead departed these lands never to return." Blain's gaze travelled to the painting. "Her leaving has caused a rift in our kingdom that we all still feel."

What kind of woman could cause that much pain?

A howl sounded outside and Redlynn's attention snapped to the entrance. She sprinted toward the sound without thinking.

"Red! Wait!" Blain yelled.

Throwing it open, she burst outside. At the gate of the drawbridge stood an enormous black Were. His golden eyes glowed into the night. They were here now. Threatening the castle. Everything else forgotten, Redlynn's instincts kicked in. She scanned the courtyard for a weapon. A wagon full of hay sat at the bottom of the steps to the right. Rushing down, she grabbed a pitchfork and made for the drawbridge.

Ten feet from the Were, she stopped suddenly. A jolt shot through her. Like the Weres in the woods, he seemed to be waiting for something. He stared at her, all too familiar. Pitch-black fur fell long from his head and shoulders. Her body quaked at the nearness of him, and something inside screamed for her to drop the pitchfork. She lunged at the beast and it backed up, biting at the pitchfork.

Instantly, Blain was at her side. He grabbed the pitchfork from her and thrust it at the giant beast. The Were growled and bared his teeth, before shifting its gaze back to Redlynn.

"Go!" Blain shouted to her. "Get inside."

She froze on the spot. The ache in her belly grew. *Not now!* Now was not the time to have to deal with female issues. Ignoring the cramping, her gaze narrowed. Something about him was so familiar. Had he been in the village? The one who killed Anya?

"Go!" Blain bellowed, grabbing her by her good arm and shaking her out of her reverie.

This had to be the Were. She needed her sword. Turning, she ran toward her room.

*****

Seeing her run out of the castle wearing that dress had not been something Adrian was prepared for. He'd been mesmerized by her beauty. Showing her resourcefulness, she'd grabbed the pitchfork. She'd make truly a magnificent mate. But not for him.

Adrian turned his attention to Blain.

"Sorry about that." Blain threw the pitchfork aside. "I had to at least let her out of her room, or she was going to end up out here in the woods. You need to talk to her soon if you're going to, Adrian. She's determined to leave. I fear one of you is going to end up dead."

He nodded his shaggy head. Blain was right, yet again. He had to tell her the truth about who he was, and about the rest of them. But he needed to time it right. She'd improved overnight. She'd hefted the pitchfork with both hands, showing little weakness in her dislocated shoulder. He had been expecting at least a week's time before she was up and about. From there he'd hoped to introduce her to the men, and see if she fancied any of them. An ache gnawed in his gut at the thought. Memories of her soft lips and the warmth of her body in his arms filled him. He grumbled. He'd spent the entire evening trying to run the memories out of his head; it hadn't worked.

"The men are still eating. They'll be out in a minute." Blain broke through Adrian's thoughts. "You should go though. I'm sure she'll return. She used her bow earlier. And even with her shaky arm, her arrow flew pretty straight."

Adrian didn't want to hurt her and he didn't want her hurting herself. A Sister like her would be a great asset in the fight against the vampires. Adrian barked.

"I can't promise to keep her in her room, but I'll at least try to keep her inside."

Blain had saved Adrian on several occasions. Even so, the thought of him and all of his charms, spending time with Redlynn, made Adrian's chest tighten. Stop it. She isn't meant to be yours. Between her and Blain, they could rule strongly, in Adrian's stead. He wished for the millionth time that the mental connection he had with his men while in wolf form worked when they were in human form. He had several choice words he was dying to say.

The door to the castle opened and four men emerged. He backed away until he reached the other end of the drawbridge. Turning, he ran into the forest, threw his head back and howled. Within a minute, four wolves appeared from the wood and shifted into human form. They each found the clothes that they'd dropped several hours earlier and dressed quickly.

"Mmmmm. I smell dinner."

"Chicken," Angus sighed, appearing through the trees.

"We'll try to save you some, Adrian," Rue laughed.

Adrian growled at the men and they took off toward the drawbridge. They passed the four newcomers, shouting tidings to each other. The four new men reached Adrian and bowed in turn. Adrian snapped his jaws and they stripped and shifted. He didn't want to be out tonight, he wanted to be spending his evening talking and lying with Redlynn.

"Let's move." His patience wore thin.

"Met Redlynn," said Bo.

"Good on ya," said Noth.

"Cut it," Adrian snapped. *"We have work to do. Besides, she isn't mine."* He tried to keep the possessive edge out of his thoughts.

"Oh, no?" asked Noth. *"She sure smelled like you'd marked her. And since she's been spending the nights with you. I just assumed..."*

"If you decide you don't want her—" Markum didn't finish his sentence before Adrian leapt at him, and the group took off into the night.

No, he wasn't attached to her at all.

CHAPTER NINE

"And where do you think you're going?" Blain leaned against the doorframe.

Redlynn tried to heave her pack over her shoulder. "I'm going after it."

"Says who?"

Her shoulders tensed. "I don't need your permission, Blain."

"Nope, you don't. But you do need Hanna's."

Just then Hanna arrived. Her motherly gaze flit from Redlynn to her pack on her shoulder and back again. Her face hardened.

"Get in bed," Hanna ordered.

"I thank you for your help, but I need to go. When I've finished my task, I'll return and you can look at me then, if you wish." Redlynn let the hint linger in the air to see if she'd be allowed to return. Leaving Wolvenglen, even with all the stares from the men, tore at her heart.

"What you need to do is get into bed and heal." Hanna crossed to the table, set down her bag, and removed Redlynn's pack from her shoulder.

"I swore vengeance against the Weres who killed my best friend, and have been taking girls from my village." Redlynn shook her head. "I don't expect you to understand. I appreciate your kindness and what you have done for me, but I have stayed too long already." She grabbed her pack with her good hand, from where Hanna had placed it.

"What about Adrian?" Blain chimed in.

"I…" her voice faltered. She wanted to say goodbye to him, but she was afraid. Afraid that if she saw his face…she'd stay. And she couldn't let any attraction she had for him stand in her way. "You tell him goodbye for me. He's a Lord, he understands duty."

Hanna stepped in her way, blocking the exit, and squeezed Redlynn's bad shoulder. She cried out and dropped her things, clutching her arm.

"If you leave now, you die. You're injured. You can't lift that sword for more than a minute, I reckon. How do you intend to kill a Were? Stand and wait for them to impale themselves on it for you? And how shaky were you when you tried your bow earlier?" Hanna jutted her chin toward Redlynn's bow.

Redlynn gripped her shoulder, holding back anger and tears, refusing to answer. She didn't like being scolded like a disobedient child.

"You can be as mad at me as you want," Hanna said, "but believe it or not, I am trying to help you, girl." She removed the pack from Redlynn's shoulder once more and set it on the table.

"Why don't you have a drink of mead and think about it for a minute?" Blain crossed to the table and picked up a goblet. He filled it and held it out to her. "We can't stop you from leaving, but we can help you wait until you are thinking more rationally."

Redlynn reluctantly took the goblet, drained it. Blain sat the cup down and moved closer to her. Too close. He laid his palm on her good shoulder and she noticed it wasn't as warm as the day before. He smiled at her. She pushed away from his touch, but he stepped forward again.

"Why are you so close to me? Adrian said I could leave whenever I want. Has that changed?"

"You're going to lie down." Hanna's voice gentled.

92

Redlynn looked between the two of them. The room swayed. Something wasn't right.

"What did you do to me?" She stepped toward the door, but stumbled.

"Come on, let's put you in bed."

Her knees wobbled. Blain grabbed her before she fell and carried her like a ragdoll to the bed.

"What the hell did you put in my drink?"

"A little something to help you relax, that's all," Blain admitted with a half-hearted smile. "Adrian really would kill me if I let anything happen to you, golden sister. And between you being mad at me, and him being mad at me, I'll choose you every time. Sorry." Then he kissed her lightly on the forehead.

"Jackass," she yelled. "I should kill you for that. You had no right."

Blain looked at her, his eyes holding sadness. "Sometimes we do things for the greater good that could be considered questionable. Given the opportunity, I'd do it again to keep you safe."

"You're wrong."

Blain shook his head. "Rarely."

Her blood pounded in her ears. He was infuriating. But there was nothing she could do about it. For now. She couldn't concentrate; sleep was close to overtaking her. At least it would help with the cramping.

"I know you don't believe us, Red, but in time you will," said Hanna. "We honestly only want to keep you from doing something you'll regret later on. There are worse things in the woods than the wolves."

"Not to me." Redlynn's mind whirled. She tried to concentrate on Hanna's face. "Why do you protect the wolves? What is it out there that you're more afraid of?"

Hanna smoothed Redlynn's hair and her brow furrowed. She put the back of her hand on Redlynn's forehead. "Are you alright?"

"I'm drugged, how am I supposed to know?" Redlynn snapped. What was going on? Was she now a prisoner? A shiver ran through her. Now more than ever she needed to get out of here. Something wasn't right with the castle.

"You feel warm." Hanna touched Redlynn again and then pulled down her dress and examined her neck. "You may have an infection. Maybe the bite healed with something inside." Hanna opened her medicine bag. Pulling the contents out, she scanned several vials. Then she sat back on the bed. "Drink this. It should help with the onset of the infection."

Redlynn scrutinized the bottle. After what Blain had just done, it could be anything. "I'll pass."

Hanna sighed. "Girl, you are more stubborn and suspicious than any Sister I've ever met. Tell me, do you really think we mean you harm?"

"No. But I do think you all want something from me; what it is, I haven't figured out yet. And there are things about this castle that don't add up. Why are there so few women? Why are all the men large and handsome and strong? Why do they still mourn the loss of a long-since dead queen? It doesn't make sense."

Hanna smiled. "Drink this. It's goldenseal and ecchinate, it should help if there's an infection. You can question us to death tomorrow and we will answer all of your questions."

Hanna's eyes appeared sincere. Redlynn sniffed the bottle and recognized the scent of the ingredients that Hanna had named. It reminded her of her mother. She parted her lips and Hanna poured the tincture down her throat.

"Rest now. Yell tomorrow." Hanna stood and drew the curtains around Redlynn's bed as she dozed off to sleep.

*****

"What do you mean she has an infection?" Adrian asked in a loud whisper. "She's healed, hasn't she?" His gaze travelled to the draw curtains. He fought the urge to go look at her.

"Yes, Lord, she has. But she has a fever I cannot explain. I can only think that something may have been sealed under her skin when the wound closed," said Hanna.

"But there's no oozing, no pustule." He bit his fingernails and paced the floor.

"No, nothing like that. It could be from the traumas she's suffered. We'll have to wait and see. I've given her something to help; hopefully it will be enough." Hanna chewed her lip. "She's very headstrong."

Adrian already knew that all too well. He stopped pacing. Hanna's gaze was heavy upon him. She'd been one of the first Sisters to return. "You have something to say, Hanna?"

"Blain had to drug her."

"What?" Adrian closed his eyes and shook his head. She'd never trust them now. "She was determined to get out of the castle. You're going to need to tell her, sire. The news will come as a shock, yes, but she's determined to find and kill you, M'lord. It's dangerous for you both."

"I know. I know." Adrian rubbed his hands over his neck. He'd tell her; as soon as the fever passed. "Thank you for caring for her, Hanna, while I was out."

"She is asking questions of all of us. Questions we aren't supposed to answer without you. But I promised her we would answer them. Tomorrow."

Adrian blinked several times. Tomorrow? Hanna had no right to tell Redlynn that.

"I know it wasn't my place. But if we don't, we'll lose her. And I don't need to tell you what's at stake."

Adrian grumbled deep in his chest. "No. You don't."

"I should go. The baby is teething and Fendrick doesn't do well with the crying."

Hanna gathered her belongings and left as Blain walked in.

"How was patrol?" he asked.

"A bloodsucker was in the wood."

Blain's eyes sparkled. "The same one?"

"Long blond hair, dark leather coat."

"That's him." Blaine turned to leave. "I'll go."

"No." Adrian waved his hand. "Angus is out there. You've done enough tonight helping with Redlynn."

"Where did you find him? The vampire."

"By the southern border."

Blain's eyes fixed on the fire.

"Go to bed, brother," Adrian said. "Tonight's been long for all of us, and patrol reminded me that we need to find the missing girls and take care of the vampires' adventures into our woods. Starting tomorrow, I am going to be counting on you to help me double the patrols."

"We'll find the girls." Blain moved to Adrian. "Even if we have to go into Tanah Darah ourselves. I'll make sure of it." The men embraced and then Blain left.

Adrian studied the closed curtains around his bed. Redlynn's breathing was deep and she snored slightly, making him smile. His wolf stirred at the thought of her in his bed. Since her arrival, his wolf was becoming what Adrian had denied for so long. He was becoming the Alpha. Protective, judicious, dominant. He didn't like it. Didn't want it, but he couldn't deny it. Redlynn made him want to be king. If something happened to her now... His ribcage and stomach muscles tightened at the thought. His heartbeat quickened and his breath caught. Leaning on the table for support, he clutched his chest. No. This couldn't be happening. He didn't want to care for her. Squeezing his eyes shut, he saw her peachy skin, her red hair, her golden eyes. He slammed his fists into the table.

"No!" he roared.

"Adrian?"

His head whipped up. He'd woken her. Breathing deeply, he ran his hands over his face and hair. He stepped to the side of the bed and slid back the curtain. She lay peaceful in the blood-red dress he'd picked for her. He was pretty sure that she'd be amazing in all the dresses he'd stored away.

Gently, he pushed a silken strand from her face.

"Where've you been?"

"I had a few things I needed to attend to."

"Blain drugged me."

"Yes, I'm sorry about that. Let me help you turn over, so you don't irritate your shoulder further."

He bent down and put his arms underneath her. The herbs Hanna had given her permeated her breath.

"Will you help me get this dress off?"

Oh no. Adrian stared at her. The desire building in his loins answered her question. "I should get Hanna."

"No, don't bother her. It's all right. I can get it myself."

Adrian swallowed hard, his breeches getting tighter by the moment.

She pushed to her feet, and swayed. He put his hand out to steady her, and she fell against his chest.

"Sorry." She looked up into his eyes and his breath caught. She straightened and leaned on the wall. "You can let go."

Adrian hadn't realized he was still touching her. He let his hand slide down the fabric of her sleeve. Her eyes were glassy.

"I'll help," he croaked. He cleared his throat and tried again. "I can help you out of your dress." His brain told him not to do it. He knelt in front of her, breathing in and out several times, trying to calm himself. He hesitated momentarily. He was about to take

97

off her clothing. A shiver of desire scuttled over his skin. He ran his hands under her dress, trying to keep his thoughts pure. Her skin was warm to the touch, even to him. Her body was definitely fighting something. Lifting her gown up over her knees, then her thighs, he stopped and dropped the hem of the dress.

"Is something wrong?" She clutched the bed for support.

Adrian stepped away, struggling to keep his wits about him. It was hard with his wolf pounding to be let loose.

"You have no undergarments." He tried to keep his voice even.

"I do, they are just shorter. I don't wear the usual female under things because I'm usually in breeches."

He tried to concentrate, but the touch of his hands on her soft, bare skin was almost more than he could take. The arousal growing within him was an unbearable thirst that needed to be slaked.

"Uh... do you have anything for me to put on you after we remove the dress?" He didn't meet her eye.

"The nightgown I wore before is in the bathing room." Redlynn swayed slightly.

Adrian moved away from her quickly, unable to control the uncomfortable bulge in his breeches. He tried to calm his mounting need. She was in no state to be taken advantage of, no matter how much his wolf wanted to claim her.

He found the gown on the floor and lifted it, taking in her scent. Rushing to the basin, he plunged his hands into the frigid water and splashed it on his face. At the shock, his wolf retreated. He took several long gulps from the pitcher, then went to the small window and threw it open. The cold breeze slapped his face and helped his head clear.

Get a hold of yourself. She is a female, a beautiful female, but she needs your help right now, not your loving. Besides, he didn't want to love her. He wanted to bed her, but he still had no interest in mating and becoming king. Adrian stared at the lights in the sky, breathing deeply for several minutes, and trying not to envision her naked body beneath his. It didn't work. He grabbed the gown and walked out. Redlynn leaned against the wall waiting.

Without a word he knelt again and lifted the crimson silk. He averted his eyes and skimmed his hands over her hips, up her sides, atop her silken shoulders, and down her arms. He tossed the gown away and grabbed the nightgown. Keeping his gaze trained on the wall, he eased the new nightgown over her, letting it drop down, covering her body. A spicy, musky scent wafted off of Redlynn's skin, so strong it made him quake with need.

"Am I so ugly that you cannot even bear to look at me?"

How in the world could she think that? He watched the way her supple, soft lips moved as she spoke. Memories of their kiss the night before stirred the wolf again. Redlynn laid her palm flat upon his chest. Her soft fingers caressed his skin.

"Adrian–"

"You should lie down."

"Lie with me."

Yes. No! Her scent filled his nostrils until he couldn't think straight. He wanted to lie with her more than anything. To feel the softness of her skin, the caress of her touch. To make her his.

"I missed you all day. Lying in your bed, smelling your scent on the pillows. I don't know why I want you so badly. I've never wanted a man before. But I want you." Stretching up on her toes, she pressed her lips to his. He stood still as her tongue skimmed over his lip, coaxing him for a response.

He lifted his hands to push her away, but before he knew what he was doing, his arms were around her, pulling her to him. Her lush body pressed into his chest and his skin tingled where her hand still lay. He opened his mouth wider to allow her access. She probed and teased his tongue with her own. The force with which she kissed him startled him. The heat of her body scorched his, and her scent made him dizzy. He lifted her, placing her on the bed.

She watched him with a glassy stare as he removed his shirt and slid under the covers on the other side of the bed.

*****

Whatever Blain had given her was making Redlynn lose her inhibitions, but she didn't care. A pulsing, aching need throbbed between her legs, and was not from being close to her woman's time. Something inside of her was awakened, and set her on fire, something that could only be sated by being near Adrian. Though she was a virgin, all she'd been able to think about was him. The feelings that had overtaken her confused her. But nothing else mattered at that moment. Her body called for him.

His hands on her skin as he'd undressed her caused her to almost explode. Redlynn found herself needing him inside of her. She slid closer to him and smelled the forest on his skin. Her mouth found his, her hands roaming his chest and stomach. His skin was smooth beneath her fingertips. She traced his hard nipples and a rumble of pleasure escaped him as he pulled her close, kissing her harder. His hands moved down her back to her rump and he crushed her body into his. This was it. The moment she'd been waiting for. To finally have a man want to make love to her. It was terrifying and exciting. She reached under the covers for the cord for his breeches, but his hand found her first.

Redlynn gazed deep into his brown eyes; golden flecks glowed within them. She was unsure. What if he didn't want her the way she wanted him?

As if answering her fears, he kissed her softly on the mouth. But she wanted more; she wanted all of him. She pulled him to her, only to have her shoulder scream in pain. Her flinch made him retreat.

"Let's just take this a bit slower." He clenched his jaw.

"I don't want to."

"Neither do I, but–"

Redlynn moved in and kissed him hard. A moan escaped his chest that she swore sounded like a dog whimper. He pushed her away.

"What? Is it me?" Her temper flared.

"No. *No.*" He peppered her face with light kisses. "We just... I can't. I don't want to hurt you."

His lips on her skin was an exquisite agony. "You won't."

Adrian sucked in a ragged breath. He ran his thumb over her lips. "You test me in ways I have never been tested, woman. But I must be chivalrous and say, no."

"I think I might burst into flames if I don't have you soon." The throbbing inside of her was an ache that, with the knowledge that she couldn't have him, had become painful. She scissored her legs, trying to stop the sensation.

"Come, let me hold you as you rest." He opened his arms.

She didn't want to be held. She wanted him inside her. She wanted him to make the pain stop.

"Trust me. I want it as much as you do." He kissed her cheek.

"Then why?" She searched his eyes for the answer, but they darkened and a frown crossed his features.

"Let me hold you." He gathered her against his chest.

Redlynn curled into his body with her head on his shoulder. She traced circles on his skin as he stroked her hair and kissed her skin. She refused to force him to do something he'd regret, and she wasn't all that sure she wanted to lay with a man she barely knew, but the throbbing inside of her was getting stronger with every moon passing. She prayed that her fever would break by the next day.

Adrian hummed a haunting tune, and soon she relaxed. What was happening to her? Her body and her mind were at war. Being in Adrian's arms both helped and made things worse. After a long while, she drifted off to sleep.

CHAPTER TEN

The next morning Redlynn tore at her gown to get it off as Adrian sprinted from the room to find Hanna. Fire scorched her skin. A pool of sweat soaked the sheets beneath her. By the time Hanna and Adrian returned, she wore nothing but her short bloomers, covered only in a thin sheet.

"What's wrong with her?" Adrian's voice held a note of worry.

"I don't know," Hanna admitted. "She looks fine."

"I don't feel fine," Redlynn moaned. "Give me something for the heat," she whimpered.

"I have nothing. We can bathe you in cold water, put a cold compress on your head, but you should know, Red, there's nothing for a fever like this. It must take its course and burn itself out."

"If it doesn't burn me out first." Her eyes felt like they were melting in their sockets. Her head pounded in her ears.

"Hanna, get the compresses." Adrian sat next to Redlynn and stroked her cheek. Her body ached for him. His hair lay loosely around his shoulders and his brown eyes were full of concern. *He's beautiful in the morning.* The throbbing inside of her increased at his touch on her skin. As irrational as it seemed, something told her that the only way to cure her was to make love to him.

"What's wrong with her now?" Blain entered the room.

"Nothing," Redlynn snapped. "I don't want you here."

Blain laughed, moving closer. "Now, now, don't be like that golden sister."

"Blain." Adrian's voice held warning. "She's sick. Step away from her."

"Is it catching?" Blain looked at Redlynn, amused. He took a deep breath and his brows furrowed.

"You drugged me. Get out!" Redlynn sat up suddenly. Her anger at his violation was enough to make her want to run him through with her sword.

Adrian was up on his feet in an instant. "Leave." He clenched his jaw.

Blain's smile evaporated. "Easy, brother." He sniffed the air again and his eyes lit on Redlynn.

She blinked several times, trying to focus on his face.

"What can I do?" Blain asked.

"Tell the women to collect as much cool water from the spring as possible. She needs to bathe."

Blain's gaze travelled to Redlynn and back to Adrian. "I'll do it."

His concern for her seemed genuine, but what he'd done to keep her inside was not something easily forgiven. No matter the reason.

Blain pressed his forehead to Adrian's. "I'd do anything for you, brother. You know that." The two men embraced in a way Redlynn had never seen men do before. A whine escaped Adrian's chest. Blain whispered something in his ear, then kissed him on the forehead and left.

"You two are close."

"He's my oldest friend. We have seen many bad times together." Adrian sat down and gently touched her. "Do you hurt?"

"My shoulder's better than yesterday. And I've had a fever before, of course, but not like this. I feel like I am burning up from the inside out. And my–"

103

"What? What is it?" His eyes searched her face.

"Nothing," she said quickly. How could she tell him that a need to lie with him grew inside her in a way that was almost all-consuming? Even his touch on her cheek was now painful.

He watched her for a moment before Hanna returned, followed by Dax, who held a large basin of water. Dax set it on the night table and Hanna brought several towels. She poured a vial that smelled strongly of eucalyptus into the basin, and then dipped in the rag.

"Keep this on her head."

"I'm not going anywhere." Adrian smiled at Redlynn and put the cool water on her brow.

The hours passed slowly, with Adrian sitting at her side and mopping her brow. Occasionally he'd check her, frown, and start mopping again. He ran the towel slowly over her arms and legs, humming again as he went.

"What are you're humming?" she asked, her throat dry and gravely.

"It's an ancient tune of love and loss. Of a wish gone wrong and of the price that was paid for arrogance."

He continued to run the towel over her limbs.

By mid-afternoon Redlynn couldn't understand why she hadn't turned to ash yet. When Blain stopped by, Adrian sent him to find Hanna.

"She's worse. We need to bathe her, Lord Adrian," Hanna declared.

Several other women entered with buckets of water. Hanna covered Redlynn with the bed sheet and Adrian carried her to the tub and stood her on shaky legs.

"We'll do it," said Hanna.

Adrian didn't move. His face was full of fear and apprehension.

Blain grasped Adrian by the arm. "Come on. Let's get you something to eat while she bathes."

Adrian seemed confused by Blain's words, but allowed himself to be led out of the room.

When the bathing room door closed, Hanna and the others removed the sheet and under things and helped her into the tub. Redlynn tried to protest the frigid water, but the women forced her in. She cried out as they poured the water over her shoulders.

"It will help," Hanna crooned. "Phina come, brush her hair to distract her."

An hour later, Phina and another woman helped Redlynn out of the tub. She shivered and her teeth chattered together. The mind-numbing cold was a stark contrast to the fire that burned her just an hour earlier. Hanna dried her with the towel, and then a new nightgown and longer pantaloons were produced. She felt wrung out and weak.

The women helped her to the bed and tucked her in. Hanna stood by and made sure she sipped from a cup of water and honey.

"Jelosa will stay with you, while I go for Lord Adrian," she said.

Redlynn nodded mutely.

Hanna touched her forehead and then replaced the cooling rag.

"Your fever is better. Let us hope it continues to go down." Hanna squeezed Redlynn's hand, and then the group of women left.

Jelosa busied herself around the room. She took the trays of food that had yet to be cleaned up and moved them into the hall. Then she picked up Redlynn's sword and set it against the wall, along with her bow and quiver. Going to Redlynn's pack she opened it and pulled out the clothes, setting them in a dresser drawer. She wanted to protest, but she didn't have the strength. Jelosa unwrapped the food items and sniffed them. A few pieces she set outside the door, presumably on the trays to be taken away.

The other food items she put back inside the pack, along with her herbs. The bedroll she set next to the quiver. Her cloak was pulled from under the table, shook out and then hung on a hook near the fireplace.

Jelosa stocked more wood on the fire and swept the room. When she finished, she pulled out a chair and sat down.

"There. That's much better. It's been a while since a female has been in here to clean up."

Jelosa was plump with brown curly hair, pulled tight into a bun. Something about her voice sounded familiar, but Redlynn was too tired to think of who it reminded her of.

"I used to hate living out of a pack," Jelosa mused, running her finger over the stitching of Redlynn's leather satchel.

"I'm used to it."

"Oh, I was used to it. But I hated it. Here, though... here I have found peace. You can find peace here, too—"

"Evening, Jelosa." Blain's cool voice floated over from the door.

Jelosa yipped and got to her feet. "Master Blain." She gave a little curtsy.

"I can sit with Redlynn."

"No," Redlynn croaked. She sipped her water.

Jelosa looked from Blain to Redlynn. "But Hanna–"

"I'll sit with her."

Jelosa nodded as Blain's gaze bore into her, hard. Then she curtsied to Redlynn. "It was nice to meet you, Lady Redlynn. I hope to see you up and well soon." She quickly left the room.

"You, too," Redlynn called after her, unsure of what had transpired between Jelosa and Blain. It sounded like Jelosa had been trying to extend her an invitation to stay in Wolvenglen. "That wasn't very nice of you. And I told you, I don't want you here."

Blain sighed and sat down in the chair by the table. He tapped on the table with his fingers and shifted his position several times before answering her. "Adrian will be here soon. He had a piece of urgent business to attend to."

"Is he alright?"

"He's fine. But he wanted me to let you know that if it weren't so urgent, he'd be here." He glanced at the door, and then out the window.

Redlynn narrowed her gaze on him. He caught her stare and gave her a tight smile. He glanced at the door again, and then produced a piece of wood and a knife from his pocket, and began to carve at it, shavings falling around him. They didn't speak more, but Redlynn watched him until her lids got heavy. The respite from her fever felt wonderful. Her only concern was Blain being so close. She reached under her pillow and felt the knife still in place. She wrapped her hand around it and closed her eyes.

*****

Adrian's mind screamed at him as he raced through the forest. The last thing he wanted was to be out on patrol, but a bloodsucker had been spotted in the woods. If they hadn't cornered it, he wouldn't be out here.

"Is he still in there?" Adrian asked.

"He hasn't come out, and there is no other exit," said Christos.

"I'm on my way."

"We aren't going anywhere," replied Angus.

"Let us go in and talk to him," said Jale.

"We can make him talk," Juda snarled.

"No one goes in but me," Adrian roared.

Adrian wanted to get in, question the vampire, kill him, and get home to Redlynn's side. Despite all of his protestations, he had feelings for her. If anything happened to her while he was gone, he would never forgive himself.

*****

When Redlynn awoke sometime later she was on fire again. Blain had pulled up his chair by the bed and slept in it with his feet up on the nightstand. *I need to get out of here. I need some air.*

When she was a girl and had a fever, her mother used to take her out into the woods and lay her on a soft bed of cool moss, sing to her, and bathe her in the nearby stream till the fever passed. She wanted nothing more than to lie in the cool stream water and moss-covered ground. Crawling to the edge of the bed, she pulled herself to her feet and headed for the exit. She'd just gotten the door open when Blain was at her side.

"What are you doing?" he asked in alarm.

"I need water," she croaked. Her throat felt like she's been eating sand for the last week.

Blain touched her arm and she jerked away from him. He stopped suddenly and sniffed her. A look of confusion crossed his face. He sniffed her again, moving closer, his pupils wide and dilated. "Crap. You need to return to bed."

"You're not my mother."

"I'm going to get you some water and Hanna."

"I need water."

"I know. And I'll get it for you." He lifted her and put her on the bed.

"Let me go."

"Don't leave this room, Redlynn. I mean it, don't leave. I can't protect you if you leave this room right now. So please, listen to me this once. I'll be back in a minute."

Her mind whirled and her heart pounded. Sweat no longer beaded on her skin. "I need air."

"I'll open the window." He moved to the wall, pushed open the glass. "Please, Red. Please stay here." His eyes pleaded with her. He rushed from the room.

Redlynn whipped her head from side to side on the pillow and moaned. A cool breeze rolled over her skin, taunting her with scent

108

of the woods. Stream water, the moss, even dirt. The woods called to her, tempting and begging her to join them.

The moon, swollen, round and white, shone brighter than she'd ever seen. A million twinkling lights teased her with their brilliance. A pain shot through her belly and up into her chest. Redlynn gasped for air as the twinge shot through her limbs.

I have to get out of here!

She stood once more and headed for the door, stepping barefoot into the hallway. Slowly she made her way toward the dining hall. She reached the balcony. Several men drank down below. Some were playing darts, others were playing cards or arm wrestling. One of the men playing cards stopped and sniffed the air.

"You smell that?" he asked.

Another man sniffed the air as well. "What is that?"

"It smells like–"

A groan escaped one of the men. "That's delicious. It makes me want to just–"

Most of the men had stopped what they were doing now, and lifted their noses into the air to sniff. *It's me!*

Redlynn melted into the cool stone wall behind her and slid sideways toward the staircase. Below, the men talked and whispered. When she reached the bottom step, she slunk as far into the shadows as possible and crossed to the entrance hall. Her heart pounded. If they found her, they'd call for Blain, and she wouldn't be able to get into the woods. She needed to go to the woods. She *needed* the river. Her mother's river.

"I think I'll see where Jelosa is." A redheaded male rushed from the room.

"Yes." Fendrick stood and rubbed his hand over his scalp. "I think... Hanna..." Then he, too, rushed from the room.

What was going on? Redlynn reached the door and slid out as Blain rushed in from the kitchen area. He stopped and sniffed the air.

"To your rooms," he barked.

The men grumbled, but they obeyed the command. Redlynn closed the door and crossed to the entrance. She stumbled and almost fell, but caught herself and kept moving. When the exterior door opened, the wind whipped into her face and she took a deep breath, filling her lungs with the night air.

"Lady Redlynn!"

The call came from behind her. It was Dax. He was going to stop her. Redlynn dashed down the stone steps. She moved too quickly and almost fell, but Dax was there and caught her. *Blast it all!*

"Lady Redlynn, what are you doing out here? You're supposed to be inside."

"I need water."

"Let me get you some."

"I need moss." She stumbled forward, trying to make her way to the bridge. Her limbs felt like oatmeal.

Dax reluctantly helped her move, glancing over his shoulder to the castle several times. "Lady Redlynn, please. I don't want trouble with Adrian and Blain."

"Just let me go to the water and moss."

"Moss? No, please–"

"Leave me," she shouted, shaking him off. "I need water!" Redlynn took several steps forward. She was almost to the gate when he rushed up to her. She spotted the pitchfork from the night before. Stooping, she grabbed it and spun around, impaling Dax in the leg. He let out an inhuman roar.

Redlynn released the pitchfork and it stuck where it was, its prongs deep in his thigh. Dax roared in pain. Blood oozed from the wound, making her stomach lurch and her head spin. "I didn't

110

mean to… I didn't…" Wide-eyed, she backed away from Dax as he clutched at his leg. Her hand flew to her mouth, stifling a cry. *What's wrong with me? I just injured a defenseless man!* "I'm sorry," she whispered. "I didn't mean to."

Dax ripped the pitchfork from his leg, bleeding heavily. "You can't go into the woods." He limped forward. "Lady Redlynn, you *can't.*"

"I need water. My mother used to take me…the moss…" she mumbled. Redlynn moved to the drawbridge, through the gate, and made for the woods. Behind her Dax screamed Blain's name.

CHAPTER ELEVEN

Adrian approached the cave with caution. Juda and Jale, already in human form, stood at the entrance. Angus and the other wolves moved away as he stood on his hind legs and shifted.

"Bloodsucker," he called into the cave.

There was no answer.

"Bloodsucker, show yourself. This is Prince Adrian of Wolvenglen, show yourself, or I'll send my wolves in to tear you apart." He was in no mood to play games.

From the depths of the cave, a shadow moved and a tall, pale figure with blond hair walked out into the mouth of the cave. He wore a leather traveling cloak and had a sword strapped to his back.

"Who are you, and why are you on my lands, bloodsucker?"

"Sageeren. My name is Sageren, not Bloodsucker. But you may call me Sage."

"What are you doing on my lands, Sage? Many of you have been here lately."

"So I've seen."

"What do you want?"

"What do I want? Or what do they want?" Sage questioned.

Adrian was in no mood. He growled. "Don't play games."

"What they want is blood. What I want is to tell you about it."

"Why?"

"Because someone in the woods is helping them get the blood. I've heard that they took some girls. Virgins."

"Who's helping them?" Adrian asked.

Sage shook his head. "That, I don't know."

"And why are you telling me this?" Adrian demanded, his patience waning.

"Because you protect the humans, specifically the girls that are being taken. I think the Weres have suffered enough at the hands of my uncle, the king. And I don't agree with what is currently being done to the humans by my kind."

"What do mean to the humans?" Adrian took a step closer to Sage. *Had they gotten through his borders into the farmlands?* "Are there more than the girls?"

Sage shifted his stance and scanned the wolves. "Let me take care of that. You just worry about your women."

"You're Lothar's son, the deposed vampire heir." It made sense.

"I am." Sage leaned casually against the cave wall.

Adrian let the news sink in. He'd heard the stories of the royal family being murdered by Philos when he took the throne from his brother. If this were the exiled Prince Sageren, this information would most likely come at a price. He may seem like a friend now, but you could never trust a bloodsucker. "So, what do you want in return for this information?"

"Your possible help in regaining my kingdom, should the time ever arise."

"I have no desire for another all out war with the vampires." Adrian crossed his arms over his chest.

"War is coming for the vampires whether you help or not. If you help, my side might stand a better chance at winning."

"And what does that do for me?"

Sage chuckled and then sighed. "I told you about the females. I should think that'd be enough. Even so, I promise that should I retake the throne, any vampire caught bringing unwilling humans into Tanah Darah will be executed."

Adrian tried to concentrate on the offer, but his thoughts continued to travel to Redlynn. "If we are able to find the girls, and they are still alive, you may call on me should you find yourself in need of support."

"But, Lord Adrian—" Juda broke in.

Adrian spun and bared his teeth. The wolf stood his ground for a moment, and then lowered his gaze.

"Thank you, Prince Adrian," Sage said. "May your woods be fruitful, and you find an end to your curse soon."

A ripple of grunts and growls ran through Adrian's pack. He turned at the sounds of a wolf shifting. Angus was on his feet. Brushing his shaggy red hair from his face, he moved to Adrian's side.

"Lord Adrian, I need to speak with you."

"What is it?" Angus was older, and deserved respect, but this was not the time.

Angus looked from Adrian to Sage and back again. "We've just been told that your..." Angus's eyes travelled to Sage. "Guest," he continued, "is in the woods."

Redlynn was in the wood. And though Sage had helped them, he was a vampire, and she was human. He turned to Sage. "Our business is concluded. You need to leave my woods immediately."

"I see that you're busy. So I will let myself out."

"Angus will escort you to the border." Adrian nodded to Angus.

"As you wish." Sage gave a slight bow. Adrian didn't have time to watch him leave, because he was already shifting. Once in wolf form, he felt Blain's presence.

"What happened?" he snarled. *"I left you in charge."*

114

"She was burning up. I went to get her a drink and she slipped out of the castle. Dax found her and tried to stop her, but she impaled him with a pitchfork."

"Is he alright?"

"He'll be fine. She got him in the leg. Hanna was patching him when I left. I think she was delirious. She kept telling Dax she wanted water and moss."

"What the hell does that mean?"

"I don't know."

"Where are you?" Adrian leapt over a felled tree.

"I'm heading to the river."

"I'll meet you there." There was a long silence as Adrian sprinted south. "Is there something else?" Dodging a snake, he ran up onto a rock, hurdled off, and landed ten feet away without a sound. Pulling air into his lungs, he tried to catch her scent. Blain was unusually quiet. "What is it?" He wasn't sure he could handle much more.

"She's in season."

"What do you mean? Women get their cycles all the time. Why is this so different?"

"I don't know Adrian, but she smells different. This isn't a woman's bleeding time, she's fertile."

"How in the world can you possibly know that?"

"All I know is when you catch her scent, it will be all you will want. No disrespect intended. But every male in the castle smelled it. I had to send them to their rooms. As bad as it is for her to be out here, it's better than her being there, trust me. The scent she's giving off."

What was going on? He stopped, stuck his nose in the air and sniffed, pulling air into his lungs again. The howl that cut through the night was something he couldn't hold back.

"You smell her."

"What the—"

"I don't know, but we better find her before someone else does."

"The Bloodsucker's gone," said Angus.

"Angus, you and the others, get to the castle. Blain, you go as well. Make sure the gate is dropped and the bridge secured. I don't want any of the men getting into the woods tonight."

"Aye," said Angus.

"I'm on it," said Blain.

Sage was gone, and the wolves were headed to the castle. Now all Adrian had to do was find her. And fast.

CHAPTER TWELVE

Adrian ran toward the scent of Redlynn, his very core answering the call that her body was sending. He ran on pure instinct, unable to understand what was going on. Finding her was his biggest priority.

His nose led him to the river. He turned north at the edge of the water and followed it toward the castle. After running for several miles, the fragrance grew so intense that he had to stop. Standing in the shadow of a large redwood, he shifted to human. He was naked, but there was nothing for it. He had no choice.

Moving easily to the bank, he walked a short way before he saw her. She lay on her back in the river, floating in her gown. But she wasn't moving. Panic rushed through him. Wading out into the water, he moved swiftly toward her.

"Redlynn! Redlynn," he called. He was almost to her when she turned slightly. "Redlynn," he whispered, lifting her into his arms and cradling her against his chest. He kissed her cheek in relief. Her skin was hot as coals. All he wanted to do was mate with her. He'd never smelled something that called to him the way her body did at that moment. Only the cold river water kept his desire in check.

Tension bunched his muscles as he held her close. He swallowed. He needed to get her to land, but out of the water, there'd be no hiding his arousal. His wolf begged for her. "What are you doing out here?"

"I needed water."

"We have water in Wolvenglen." The relief of finding her and the terror of her condition collided inside. His heart pounded as he held her close and kissed her cheek. He couldn't concentrate.

"My mother used to bring me to the river."

"My mother used to do the same for me," he said. "Only she did it in the tub. Come, let me take you somewhere safe, where Hanna can look after you."

"I miss her so much." She stared into his eyes. Her chin quivered and Adrian pulled her close and kissed her hair.

It had been years since he'd let in the pain he felt at the loss of his own mother, but holding Redlynn in his arms, hearing her own sorrow, brought it all back.

"She was so wonderful. Amazing and strong. She didn't deserve what happened to her. She didn't deserve to be married to my father, or have a daughter who was an outcast. She deserved better."

He looked her in the eyes. The sorrow of her life seemed to be spilling out. Everything she'd ever been through, all of the jeers and taunts. The unmet expectations and pain. How could someone so beautiful have been treated so poorly?

He shook his head. "You're wrong. She did deserve you. How you see yourself... I wish you could see yourself through my eyes."

"Lay me on the moss," she whispered.

"Redlynn—"

"Please, Adrian. Lay me on the moss. Let me see the stars and remember my mother."

He didn't want her to stay out here, but maybe it was better that she did; the scent she was giving off was dangerous—dangerous for both of them. He was barely holding back his instinct to take her and make her his mate, and he was stronger than most. Some of his men wouldn't be able to withstand.

"Your eyes are golden again," she whispered. Lifting a hand she stroked his cheek. "Why are they like mine?"

His chest tightened. He wanted to tell her, but he honestly didn't know why her eyes were like his, or why she saw his wolf eyes when he was in human form.

"Let me carry you to the moss." He was naked and without a horse, what else could he do? For all of his parents' counsel, his years of learning, tutelage and reading, nothing had prepared him for something like this.

Her body was weightless in his arms as he carried her out to the bank and laid her on a patch of moss. Above them, the clouds covered the moon. He sat next to her and swallowed down a whimper. He was sure that she'd be dead from fever before morning. Her eyes weren't focusing clearly, and she blinked at him slowly.

Hot, moist tears stung his eyes. He refused to cry in front of her, but the despair inside him was like nothing he'd known. He'd gotten too close, even though he'd promised himself he wouldn't. The pit in his stomach was only going to get worse after her passing.

"You're naked," she said after a while.

"Uh...Yes, I am." He crossed his legs and hung his head.

"Why?"

Tell her! Tell her the truth!

She turned her head to stare upward. "Have you ever stared up at the stars before? I've never seen them so bright."

"Every night when I run I look at the stars." *What does it matter now if she is going to die? Tell her.*

"Do you run every night?"

"Yes. There's a grove not far from here. When you're well I'll take you there. You can lie in the tall grass and see all of the stars

119

above. We'll go there and I'll show you the patterns I make with them. There's a dragon and a warrior. Mage towers and a giant cow."

He looked over at her and his chest clenched. She looked worse. Her cheeks were as red as strawberries and her eyes as glassy as a pool of water.

"And I'll show you the giant castle where I used to dream I'd live. And the giant bird that used to carry me there." She stared up into the trees. "There's nothing more lovely than the stars."

"There's one thing."

Her gaze turned upon him. Her eyelids closed and then opened again slowly. Pain marred her features.

"I ache for you," she said, her voice husky and low.

"And I for you," he whispered. Gods in the heavens, he wanted her like he'd never wanted a woman before.

"Then why, Adrian? Why will you not make love to me?"

"Because I am trying to be a gentleman." He tried to concentrate on anything but the desires rushing through him. Her body called to him like a siren's song. And her words only made it worse.

"I don't want a gentleman. I want you." She laid her hand on his arm.

Her slender fingers felt like candle flames licking his skin. Leaning near her, he picked up her hand, kissed it, and then each delicate fingernail. Turning her hand over, he kissed her palm, and up her wrist. The silence of the forest was like a cocoon. Her scent drifted on the breeze, invading him.

"Ever since I first laid eyes on you, I have been drawn to you. But these past two nights, it has become a pain that I cannot understand."

He trailed light kisses up her arm. He didn't want to think, just feel.

120

"The pain, the need inside of me, it's excruciating. Like I'm going to explode if I don't have you. Please, Adrian, make it stop."

Her words flooded into him. The breathy way she called his name was all it took. There was no stopping him now. If she were going to die, he'd have her die knowing that he cared. Tomorrow, he knew he'd regret it if he didn't. A tear dripped from his eye, and he kissed the crook of her elbow. Lifting her arm, she twined her fingers through his hair. They locked eyes.

The walls around his heart crumbled to pieces. Looking into her eyes, he saw it. Redlynn should have been his mate, and he'd give her whatever she asked.

He kissed up her arm to her collarbone. Peppering her, he kissed from her neck to her earlobe, down her jaw to her blistering lips. Tasting her hot breath, Adrian rolled on top of her. A groan escaped him, followed by a soft mewl from her. His arousal grew and pressed between them.

He kissed down the other side of her throat, moving her gold locket out of the way. She moaned his name when he reached the peaks of her breasts. Her hands grabbed his shoulders and her nails dug into his back, causing a rumble to escape his chest. His hand ran roughly over her thin gown, down her side, to her protruding hipbones. Digging his fingers in, he pulled her near and lifted her leg, wrapping it around his waist. He needed her.

*****

Redlynn's mind spun as Adrian kissed her body. The throbbing between her thighs had become a pain almost too much to bear. She didn't understand what was going on between them, but one thing was for sure: he was hers.

A shiver ran through her as his hands trailed down her side and rested on her hipbone, squeezing it hard. A hum of pleasure spread through her. His touch excited and teased her, making her moan with desire. He wrapped her leg around him and his excitement pressed against her. She opened her eyes. The clouds parted and the moon shone in the night sky.

Pushing up her nightgown, he reached for the waist of her undergarments. His fingers splayed flat across her belly. Something inside her twisted and she pulled away from him in shock, gasping for air.

"What is it?" he begged, searching her face.

"Pain," she gasped. The twisting tightened and she cried out.

"Where? Where do you hurt, my love?" His gaze raked over her as she clutched her stomach and curled into a ball on her side.

The pain spread up to her chest and she squeezed her eyes shut, to block it out. Her heart beat wildly. She tried to suck air into her lungs, but it was like sucking water in instead. A presence, something inside of her, was trying to claw its way out. A cracking sound reverberated through her, and Redlynn screamed in terror, grabbing her chest.

"Adrian!"

He'd stepped away from her, staring in horror, watching her suffer. Redlynn's nails lengthened and her hands shortened. The next crack flipped her onto her stomach on all fours. She screamed again at the snap of the bones in her legs. She fell on the moss. *I'm dying. Why am I dying?*

"What the– Redlynn!" came Blain's voice, as he ran out of a clump of trees and to her side.

"Blain," she whispered. "Help me."

*****

Adrian watched helplessly. This couldn't be happening. It wasn't possible. No female wolf had been born. Ever. It wasn't—

"Adrian! Wake up!" Blain yelled, cradling Redlynn in his arms. "She's shifting. She needs you."

Adrian's wolf barged through, pushing him to action. He shifted quickly and once in wolf form, Adrian heard her thoughts.

What's happening to me? I'm dying. Let me die. Make the pain stop, please gods let me die.

Adrian stepped over to where Blain held her and pushed his heavy shaggy head between them. Blain moved away and began to shift. Another bone snapped and broke, and Redlynn cried out. She was delirious with pain now, her words no longer making sense.

"Redlynn," Adrian tried to call to her. He laid his large body next to hers as she writhed and screamed. *"Redlynn, you're alright. You can do this. Let her out, let the change happen."* Adrian's heart raced. Moments before, he thought he would lose her to the fever. But now he feared losing her to her first shift. *"I'm right here."* He nuzzled her. He traced each break of her bones, each whimper, each scream. For the first time in a decade, he raised prayers to the gods. *Please let her live. Let her stay. She's the one. My one. If you let her, I'll fulfill my destiny. I'll become king. Please, don't take her now.*

In the last moments of the change, her eyes opened and locked on his. Adrian concentrated on the sound of her heartbeat, pounding too loud in her chest. *Please let her stay.*

"Adrian," was the last thing she whispered before long red hair sprouted over her body. Her snout and teeth lengthened. Her body stilled and her heart stopped.

Adrian held his breath. *Please!* There had never been a female wolf before, and many young males didn't even make it through the pain of their first shift.

A moment passed, and then another. She didn't move. Adrian held his breath and waited. *Come on, Redlynn.*

"She'll make it," said Blain.

Her chest rose as she sucked in a lung full of air. The steady pace of her quicker wolf heartbeat drummed in her chest.

Adrian howled. She'd made it through the shift. *She'll be alright now.* And now they'd be together. Forever. *Thank you,* he prayed. Fear wracked him at the prospect of becoming mated, and king. Adrian pushed his fears aside. It didn't matter now.

She lay very still for several minutes, with him nuzzling and fawning over her. Adrian could hardly wait to speak with her. To finally have her know the truth about him and about herself.

"Redlynn. Redlynn, dearest."

She blinked several times and was on her feet quick as lightning, her teeth bared. Her hackles raised and she showed no signs of knowing him.

"Redlynn, listen to me—"

A growl grew in her throat, and before he could react, she was on him. Teeth bared, she gnashed and snapped at him.

"Redlynn! Stop!"

"She can't understand." Blain stepped closer. *"Get away from her!"*

Adrian struggled with the attacking Redlynn. Blain was on her in an instant. He knocked her to the side and stood between them. Blain bared his teeth, and Redlynn growled and lunged. Blain snapped at her front leg, causing her to yelp.

"Don't hurt her," Adrian bellowed, knocking Blain aside.

"She doesn't know who you are."

Adrian moved forward and stood directly in front of Redlynn. She was almost as large as he and Blain were. Her golden eyes glowed at him in the moonlight.

*****

Redlynn knew that something was different about herself, but she couldn't figure out what. She didn't have time. Weres stood before her. And from the smell of the black one, he was the king, the one she'd wanted. Her sense of smell was on overload. It was overwhelming and frustrating. *"I'm going to kill you, you bastard! For what you did to the girls. To Anya! To my mother."*

"Redlynn, listen to me."

124

She heard Adrian, but she didn't see him. And for some reason, her voice wasn't working the way it should. She wondered if she were dreaming.

"You're going to be alright."

This was her chance. She had to kill the Were king. But he had a guard and she was weaponless. This is not the time. Redlynn scanned the area for Adrian, but he was gone. Turning on her heels, she fled into the woods. She needed to live until tomorrow. Then she'd return, well-equipped.

Redlynn ran with a speed she'd never before possessed. The trees around her were a blur as she sprinted through them. The thrill was exhilarating. She hadn't experienced the woods like this before. As she ran, she knew where every bird huddled in its nest, where every squirrel hid in its hollow, and where every deer ran from her in fear. She smelled the moss and the leaves and the water from the river.

After running for minutes, she decided that because of the fever, she had passed out and was having an incredibly vivid dream. Or perhaps the fever had claimed her life.

She didn't care. She just wanted to run, and keep running and never stop. Though she might be dead, for the first time Redlynn felt alive.

CHAPTER THIRTEEN

"We should go after her."

"No." Adrian was confused and hurt. She was a wolf, his wolf, but she'd attacked him. He'd tried to communicate with her, the way he did with his men, but it hadn't worked. Had she even heard him? Something wasn't right. Maybe it was the fever. Maybe the gods were playing a cruel trick on him for having abandoned them so long ago.

Blain bumped against him and stood his white shaggy body directly in Adrian's view. *"She's yours. This doesn't change that. She's strong, and even stronger-willed. You need to follow after her. Find her, run with her. Explain to her who we are. Who she is."*

Adrian hesitated. *"No."*

"Don't be foolish, what if she gets lost, or injured? She isn't from these woods. She doesn't know her way around here."

He was cursed after all. Just as his father had been. He swallowed down the ache inside. *"She'll be fine."*

"And what if the Bloodsucker comes back?"

"Then I wish him good luck against her." Adrian turned from Blain. His heart, heavy with pain and doubt, felt like a boulder in his chest. She hadn't even recognized him. If he went to her now, why would it be any different?

Blain lunged and bit Adrian on the ear, causing him to growl and snap back.

"Don't do this. Don't shut down."

Adrian turned again and walked away. If she was his, she'd return to him. Something in the way she'd attacked him had pierced him in the heart.

"Fine," Blain called. *"If you won't go after her, I will."* *Blain rushed off in the same direction that Redlynn had.*

"Blain! Come back!"

"You aren't my king," Blain mocked.

Adrian snarled and jetted off after him.

"If you don't want her, then maybe she'll be more amenable to me," Blain taunted again.

"If you find her, I am going to enjoy watching her rip you apart."

"You're just sore because she didn't try to kill me."

Adrian caught a glimpse of Blain's haunches as he rounded a tree and headed toward a clearing.

"When I catch you–"

"If you catch me, what? You going to maul me? Or nibble my tail?"

Adrian howled; the anger inside of him rising at an alarming rate. He wasn't sure if he was angry because of Blain's words, or at Redlynn for her stubbornness.

When he caught up several miles later, it was because they were at the edge of a clearing and Blain stopped to watch the scene. Redlynn sat in the dark of night under the moon, staring up at it. She howled. The sound was cut short as she looked around frantically.

"She doesn't understand," said Blain.

Adrian watched her circle the ground, then lie on the ground and roll in the tall grass.

"Can't you see? She doesn't realize that she's a wolf. That's why she attacked you."

She rolled in the tall grass. She looked so happy as her tail wagged.

"Call to her." Blain prodded.

Adrian waited and watched as she rolled over and over and then stopped, watching the moon high above. He wanted to go to her, to lie with her under the moon and listen to her heartbeat next to his. But he'd called to her, and she hadn't listened before. Swallowing, he made up his mind and took a step closer. Now that he'd let her in, he couldn't just let go.

"Redlynn?" he called. Her head popped up. *"Redlynn can you hear me?"*

She was on her feet scanning the glade.

"Say something."

Again, she didn't answer. Maybe Blain was right, maybe she couldn't communicate with him.

There was a rustle of trees on the other edge of the clearing, and suddenly a young girl struggled into the glade. Redlynn turned to her.

The girl appeared pale and weak. She wore a torn, dirty nightgown, her hair was unkempt, and she appeared totally delirious. Redlynn moved to the girl quickly, but the girl spotted her and backed up, screaming and trying to get away. Redlynn followed, uncomprehending.

"Redlynn! Redlynn!" Adrian called.

She looked around again, but then followed the girl.

"Blain! Distract her, I'll get the girl."

"Maybe you should–"

"No! She didn't try to attack you. You go after her."

Adrian shifted to human form and smacked Blain on the rump. *"Go!"*

Blain hesitated, but then darted across the clearing. The growling started as he ran across the glen. Adrian's wolf fought for control, the need to protect Redlynn from the fight his only desire. Adrian fought the beast down and entered the tree line to find the girl backing toward a large rock, and Blain and Redlynn fighting for all their worth. The girl screamed and tried to get away from the snarling, blood-thirsty wolves, but she couldn't. Adrian froze, unsure what to do. The girl didn't know him. And he was naked. He needed to get Redlynn out of the way.

"Knock her out," he bit out, his wolf protesting at the thought.

Blain stared at Adrian for a moment.

"Do it!"

Blain turned to Redlynn, just as she charged. The girl's gaze lit on Adrian and she screamed louder. Blain rammed Redlynn, and in an instant, it was over. She hit a boulder, knocked into the girl and both were out cold. Blain shifted to his human form and stood panting, bleeding from a cut above his eye. The scratches on his back oozed, and a bite on his arm was already sealing shut.

"You're welcome." He spit blood from his mouth.

"You'll live." Adrian rushed past him to check on Redlynn.

He knelt at her side and watched her shift. Her curled up, peachy body emerged beneath the retracting red fur. There was a cut to her lip and a bruise on her chest, where Blain had rammed her. Her shoulder looked like it was okay though, surprisingly enough. Blain joined him at her side.

The young girl clutched a dirty blanket. Adrian pulled it from her limp grasp and wrapped it around Redlynn.

"I tried not to hurt her too bad."

"We need to take them both to the castle."

"Where did she come from?" Adrian mused. He stood, listening for sounds of other people, but heard nothing. "Let's get

129

them back before they wake." He lifted Redlynn into his arms. Turning, he noticed Blain staring at the girl. "What's wrong?"

"Nothing," he said. "It's just... do you think?"

Hope lit in Adrian. "It has to be. You were right. The girls are still alive."

Blain picked up the girl and joined Adrian. When they reached the gate, Adrian called up for it to be opened. Hanna waited for them at the castle entrance.

She touched Redlynn's skin. "Her fever broke." Hanna moved the blanket and looked at Adrian sternly. "She's unclothed, my Lord."

"It's a long story."

"Take her to bed, I'll send someone up with a new gown," she said.

"There's another girl." Adrian nodded to the unconscious body in Blain's arms.

Hanna's brows knit together, and she walked to check the girl. Moving the girl's hair out of her face, Hanna gasped. Trickles of dried blood caked the girl's neck and arms. "Vampires,"

Blain and Adrian exchanged a look.

"We don't know," Adrian said finally. "But possibly." He didn't need the rumors getting out quite yet. He needed a chance to talk to Redlynn first. To explain the truth about Wolvenglen and about herself, before they dealt with telling the rest of the castle about the missing girls. One problem at a time.

"Bring her to my room," said Hanna.

"Maybe it'd be best if someone else did that," suggested Adrian.

"Why– Oh!" said Hanna. "Yes, I suppose you should retrieve some pants first. Fendrick would be hard to convince."

"Let me take care of Redlynn, and I'll bring clothes for both of us." Adrian headed off.

He climbed the stairs quickly, careful not to bump Redlynn as she lay limply in his arms. Reaching his room, Dax rushed toward him.

"Oh, you found her." His voice filled with relief. "I am sorry, Adrian."

"Not your fault. Not even I would've been able to stop her. Get the door, please."

"Of course." Dax passed and pushed open the door.

Adrian stalked to the bed and set Redlynn down. Removing the dirty blanket, he covered her with the duvet.

"So it's true, then. She's a she-wolf. The first of her kind... like me."

"Yes." Adrian studied Dax for a moment, who was trying to not look at Redlynn. "Can you smell her?"

Dax's eye shifted to Redlynn's sleeping form. "Yes."

"Do you...That is..." Adrian wasn't sure how to phrase it.

"I can tell that her scent is different, but it isn't near as strong as it was an hour ago. I can tell that she's fertile, but I have no desires toward her, if that is what you are asking."

"Stay with her until I return." Adrian blew out a heavy breath. "Let no one in, unless it's me or another female."

Dax nodded. "I understand."

Adrian threw open the wardrobe and pulled out a pair of breeches for himself, a pair for Blain, and two tunics. He dressed as he walked from the room.

Taking the steps two at a time, he made his way down to the front hall where Blain stood holding the girl. Staring down into the child's sleeping face, he hadn't moved from the spot where Adrian had last seen him.

"Let me take her." Adrian handed over his spare clothes.

Blain held the girl close and Adrian wasn't sure he was going to let her go.

"What is it, my brother?"

131

Blain looked up, his expression pained.

"I know. I know." Adrian set his hand on his friend's shoulder. "It's unimaginable that one of our own would cause such pain on innocent girls."

"How did she escape? How did she make it so far?" Blain mused, looking at the girl.

"Sheer will, I suppose. She's from the Sisterhood, after all. Let me take her." Adrian slid his arms under the girl. She weighed no more than a pup. "Go, brother. Go and get washed. And then you and I will have a drink together and figure out what to do next."

Adrian pounded on Blain's door ten minutes later. Blain answered it, a bottle already in his hand. He took a long swig, staring at Adrian, and then offered him the bottle. Adrian took it and drank deep.

Blain hadn't put on his shirt. The scratches on his back were already healed.

"So, the girl..." Blain's voice filled with the dread that Adrian felt.

"She's in pretty bad condition. Hanna said she's very anemic. A few more weeks, and she would've been dead. She's been fed on by the bloodsuckers for months."

"Is she awake?"

"No." Adrian shook his head and took another swig. "She needs rest, but when she's strong enough, we'll try to get her to show us the way to where she was held."

"What about Red?" Blain took the bottle from Adrian and drank again.

"What about her?"

Blain let out a bitter laugh. "Are you joking, Adrian? She's a freaking wolf!" Blain's eyes narrowed. "You have to tell her."

"You think I don't know that?" He plopped down heavily into Blain's overstuffed chair. "But how?"

"I don't know. 'Hello sweetheart, you know that fever you had, well it was actually you going into heat and shifting for the first time, because, well, you're a wolf.'"

"Great, Blain. Marvelous idea."

Blain took another large swallow from the bottle. His face grew serious. "It's the truth."

"And how many women have you met who ever wanted to hear the truth?" Adrian stared at the floor. "Tonight I thought she was going to die, and all I could think was that she'd never have known that I cared."

"She's the one from the prophecy, Adrian. I've been telling you that for days. She will bring an end to the reign of the Bloodsuckers. You need to take her to mate so she can fulfill her destiny. Then you can go out together and find the rest of the girls and bring them home. You'll be a hero and a king. That's what your father always wanted."

"How do you know what my father wanted for me?"

Blain closed his eyes and rubbed his face. "Because before he died, he made me promise to help you fulfill your destiny. To become king and bring the Sisters back. That's your destiny." He pointed to the door. "That's her destiny. Take her, make her yours. Become king."

The men stared at each other, and then Adrian shook his head. "Her destiny is her own, it's not mine to force. She needs to fulfill it in her own time."

Blain hurled the bottle at the wall. It shattered on the stone, and mead and glass rained down behind Adrian. Adrian sprang to his feet.

"What the hell, Blain?"

"How many years have we suffered, Adrian?" Blain yelled. "How many years have we suffered to protect the humans from the

Bloodsuckers because of your father's betrayal? How many brothers have we lost? And we still have no mate to bear us young? You can end this. You always could. Your fear and selfishness has kept happiness from us all. Just like your mother."

Adrian's anger boiled over. He was up on his feet, crossed the room in one stride, and punched Blain in the mouth. Blain spat on the floor, his eyes locked on Adrian's. "Take her. Become the king you are meant to be. Then together we will find the girls, return them to Volkzene, and show them the truth. It's time, Adrian, to bring our mates home."

Adrian burned with anger. All these years he'd tried so hard not to end up like his father, and all this time, he'd been just like his mother. Adrian straightened his back. Too long he'd stood in the shadows, content to be half a man. He'd not kept his promise to his father. He'd not kept his promise to his men. But no more. He needed to root out the men responsible for taking the girls of the Sisterhood, and fortify his ranks. It was time for him to become King.

CHAPTER FOURTEEN

Redlynn stood in the courtyard of the castle, taking in everything around her. She breathed the fresh air deeply and let it wash through her. Moisture drenched her nostrils and caused her dress to cling to her skin. It was going to rain. She smelled the forest beyond the gates, the hay from a nearby wagon, the dirt beneath her bare feet.

Her eyes flexed and focused easily on things she would never have been able to see before the fever. Her sight locked onto a bird sitting in a nest a hundred yards away in the trees. Turning, she watched a mouse scurrying up the side of a castle wall. A man and his wife stood on the other side of the courtyard having a hushed conversation and Redlynn heard every word.

All around her, the courtyard buzzed with a life she hadn't experienced before. A blacksmith hammered away somewhere to her left. Horses in stables whinnied and pawed at the ground. Several women scrubbed clothing in large washbasins, chattering and singing merrily.

Redlynn was amazed and confused at the same time. The only thing she could attribute it to was the fever.

Thunder cracked above her and a droplet of water hit her hair. She smiled. The couple in the courtyard and the washing women gathered their things and moved quickly inside the castle. She opened her arms wide and welcomed the rain.

As fat, glistening droplets hit her face, she laughed and covered her mouth. She felt alive and connected to everything around her. Something inside her wanted to tear out the gate and run through the woods naked. She laughed again, and again covered her mouth. She'd not laughed in such a long time that the sound of it was foreign to her ears.

Suddenly her laughter was uncontrollable. Once she started, she found that she couldn't stop. Something had happened between developing the fever and its breaking that left her feeling better than she ever had.

The crushing weight of her life was being lifted. Years of loneliness and pain melted away with each laugh. Her eyes teared and her laughs turned to weeping, allowing her to release what she'd bottled up inside for too long. The deaths of her family members and loved ones. The abandonment by her father, the feelings of worthlessness; all this and more left her body with each sob. Visions of her lonely life at the Sisterhood played in her mind as she looked around the castle. Warmth spread through her, peace and a sense of belonging replaced every bad memory. The rain picked up, washed over her. She'd been reborn.

Her laughing continued until she had to bend over to grab her aching side, trying to catch her breath.

"Redlynn! Redlynn! What's wrong?" Blain was at her side, trying to grab onto her. "What the– Are you laughing?"

"Yes." She nodded.

"What's so funny?"

"I've never laughed before." She gasped for air as chortles escaped her.

"What? I don't…" He stared at her like she'd grown a second head. "You should come inside; Adrian's a mess because you're missing again." He tried to take her by the arm.

Another voice blasted through her laughter.

"Redlynn! What's going on? Are you alright?" Adrian lifted her up by the arms. Tears flowed down her cheeks and he wiped at them with his hands. "What's wrong? What happened? Blain, what did you say to her?"

"Nothing." Blain shrugged. "She's laughing."

Adrian looked at her, confused. "What?"

"Laughing. She's laughing. She said it was funny that she's never laughed before."

"That doesn't make any–"

She wanted nothing more than to be in Adrian's arms. She took a deep breath, pushed herself up on her toes, and tackled his lips with her own. He stiffened, but then wrapped his arms around her; he lifted her off the ground as his lips parted, and she found his tongue with hers. Something inside her clicked. She was meant for this, for him. She was meant for something more than just killing Weres. She was meant to love Adrian.

He pulled away, leaving her breathless. Redlynn smiled, really smiled.

He smiled back.

"I thought you were going to die last night." His voice strained with emotion.

"Me, too," she said. "There were moments when I wished I were dead."

When he kissed her again, passion ran through her, making her quake with desire. Fat raindrops soaked through their clothes, making them cling to each other.

"You two are going to drown out here if you don't come inside," Blain called from the entrance of the castle.

Redlynn hadn't even noticed his leaving. Adrian set her down, took her hand, and ran to the castle entrance. When inside, he turned and brushed the water droplets from her face.

"What were you doing out there?"

137

"I don't know. I woke up and felt so much better that I just had to go outside. It was weird, I had the strangest dream. I dreamed I went out into the woods and lay in the river like my mother used to do with me. Then you showed up and pulled me from the water. But." She stopped.

"But what?" he pressed.

"You were naked." She fell silent, remembering her dream. The sensations of pain made her skin prickle. "I was in excruciating pain, and then–"

"What? Then what?" he asked urgently.

Should she tell him? Would he laugh? "Free," she whispered. "I was free. It was so vivid. I ran and ran. I can still remember lying under the moon. It was like you said. How you feel when you run in the forest and for the first time since my mother's death I feel it again."

"Feel what?"

"Home." She waited for him to respond.

He smiled.

"And this morning when I got up, I smelled everything; the trees and the dirt and the sky. My eyesight is amazing, so is my hearing. It is the strangest and most wonderful thing. I have no idea what the fever did to me to make me feel... like me. It's bizarre but for the first time I truly feel this is who I am meant to be."

When he didn't respond embarrassment flooded her.

"It's silly," she said.

"Do you remember anything else?" Blain leaned casually against a statue.

A wave of distrust ran through her at the sight of Blain. "Of my dream? Not really."

"It doesn't matter." Adrian gave Blain a pointed look and hugged her close. "I'm just glad that you're better."

A scream rang out from somewhere inside the castle, and Adrian and Blain turned.

"What's that?" asked Redlynn.

"A girl," Adrian replied. The three of them proceeded down a side hallway.

Redlynn had never been in this part of the castle before; it was several long hallways of stone, with wall sconces and wooden doors along one side.

There was another scream, and then another. Quickly, Adrian dragged her past room after room. Doors opened and men peered out. At the end of the hall, a large group of men gathered.

"Let us through," Adrian called.

The men parted and Redlynn took in the scene. It was a large room. Hanna stood inside. Her children were huddled in the corner with Fendrick. A girl sat on a small bed, terrified. She was dirty, wild-eyed and screaming. Hanna tried to soothe her, but it seemed futile. On the other side of the bed, a second woman spoke to the girl, but every time she did, the girl screamed louder.

"Get away! Get away!" The girl clutched the sheet and backed into the headboard.

"Lizzy. Lizzy it's me, Clara, your sister," the woman crooned.

Letting go of Adrian's hand, Redlynn stepped into the room. The girl's eyes travelled to Redlynn and she cried out, jumping from the bed.

"Red! Red! Help me!" Lizzy screeched, running to Redlynn and throwing her arms around Redlynn's waist. "Don't let me die. I don't want to go into the woods and die like my sister, Clara. Make her spirit leave me alone."

Redlynn's gaze travelled from woman to woman. The women watched her apprehensively. She moved Lizzy to arms-length and looked into her face. Realization dawned on Redlynn. Lizzy. She'd been the first taken.

"You're alive." She couldn't believe it. Redlynn reached her arms around Lizzy awkwardly and held the girl close. Lizzy's body shook with a fear Redlynn had never known.

139

She looked from Clara to Hanna. A flash of memory hit her with force. Hanna at her hut. Her mother talking to her about herbs from the forest. In an instant she remembered.

"You." Redlynn's voice hardened and ice gripped her heart. They'd lied to her. "You're Sahanna Thrist." Her gaze travelled to the other woman watching her. "And you're Claretta Metlock. You're members of the Sisterhood."

Lizzy clung to her. Redlynn's mind raced with questions, but she voiced none of them. Instead, she walked silently to the dining hall. Along the way, Hanna and Clara, who followed behind, pulled women out of their rooms.

Men filled the dining hall. Upon seeing all the women gathered, most stood and moved out of the room. Only two remained. Two men with long, dark hair and hard faces stared at the assemblage. Their eyes rested on Redlynn and Lizzy, and they exchanged a look.

"The women need the room," Adrian said.

The men didn't move.

"Jale, Juda, get out," he commanded.

Slowly they stood, taking their mugs of ale with them.

Hanna and the women sat down silently at a long table. Redlynn, Lizzy and Adrian sat opposite them on the other side. Blain stood, watching the outer door.

Redlynn's gaze travelled from face-to-face of the women gathered in the dining hall. Close up, she recognized several of them now. All former members of the Sisterhood, all had left Volkzene and never returned. There were four or five older than Hanna that Redlynn didn't know, but Clara, Hanna and several others she'd seen in Volkzene. In training classes, or around the village on patrol, but they'd all lived there.

"I don't understand." She finally vocalized what had been running through her mind for the past several minutes. "What are you all doing here?"

Hanna's gaze settled on Adrian, his body ripe with tension. He took her hand, sending a chill through her.

"There are things in the world. Things that prey on humans," he said.

"Weres," she said.

"No," said Hanna. "Not wolves; other things."

"Vampires," Lizzy whispered.

"Yes." Adrian nodded.

Redlynn hadn't misheard Lizzy, but no one contradicted the girl. It wasn't possible. "There hasn't been a sighting of a vampire in hundreds of years," she said.

"Vampires live to the north of the woods," Adrian began. "A thousand years ago, Fairelle used to be a single kingdom, ruled by King Isodor. He had four sons who each wished to rule the kingdom after the death of their father. Using an ancient mage book, they called forth a djinn from Shaidan. The djinn granted them each a wish, but twisted it to his own purposes. The first wished to be bloodthirsty in battle. The second wished for the never-ending loyalty of his men. The third wished to be able to control the elements. And the last brother wished to rule the seas. Vampires, werewolves, fae and nereids." Adrian paused. "But the brothers had called the djinn forth too many times, and the djinn was able to break free, opening a rift in what once was the heart of Fairelle, what is now the Wastelands."

Redlynn's tried to grasp his words. She'd heard parts of the legend before, but never like this. She thought it was just an old story. But the way Adrian told it made it real. Surely it wasn't possible. Humans turned into creatures by the wishes made to a daemon? It made no sense. But then again, werewolves were real.

"Red," said Hanna. "The wolves, or werewolves as we were taught by the Sisterhood, aren't bad. They protect us."

"No." She dropped Adrian's hand and stood from the table.

"Redlynn, listen, please," pleaded Adrian.

141

"They protect us from the vampires." Hanna rose.

"No, they don't!" Lizzy screeched, running to Red's side again. "They took me."

"Tell us what happened, child." Adrian's gaze shifted to Blain, who'd moved forward to the table and sat.

Lizzy began to shake again. Redlynn held her close, for her own comfort as much as for the child's.

"Come, Lizzy," Hanna prompted. "Tell us what happened that night."

Lizzy stayed silent for a long moment. "I was asleep in my bed. A howl awoke me, but I was so frightened, I couldn't move. I heard the door open; I know I should have screamed, but I couldn't. A giant brown wolf stuck his head in. Even from where my bed sat in the next room, I heard him breathing. My room faced the front door, so I saw him perfectly in the firelight. His body was huge. I'd never seen a Were before. A second brown Were came in, as well." Lizzy took a shuddered breath before continuing. "Then a man walked in. Tall and thin with long hair. The man pushed the Were aside and looked right at me. There was something in his eyes that, even though he stood by the door, I could tell he wanted me to go to him. I tried to stay in my bed, but my body wouldn't obey. When I got into the front room, he smiled. He had long, sharp teeth that grew. I'd never been so scared before. Then he bent down and smelled my neck."

Lizzy broke off and buried her tear-streaked face in Redlynn's gown.

Vampires were real? Her heartbeat quickened. What else was out there that she didn't know about? It didn't matter. It proved her right. The Weres were evil. "See?" Redlynn yelled. "How can you say the Weres protect, when you have a witness right here to their atrocities?"

"No!" Adrian rose from his seat, shaking his head vehemently. "It isn't like that. The wolves protect humans."

142

"Adrian, are you calling this girl a liar?" she shot back. She couldn't believe Adrian was trying to tell her that the Weres weren't a threat.

Adrian sighed and rubbed his temples. "It isn't as simple as you think."

Redlynn finally saw the truth of the situation. The women loved the men. The men could only live here, in the woods, uninjured by the Weres if they were in league with them. She held tightly to Lizzy as she walked backward toward the stairs.

"What do you do? You ally yourselves with beasts to keep your castle safe? You allow innocent girls like Lizzy to be taken so that you may fish and read and prosper?" Redlynn looked over the group. "You disgust me," she spat. "And you." Her gaze pierced Clara. "You still side with the Weres, knowing now what they've done to your sister?"

She couldn't believe it. She'd stayed here, in his bed. She'd fallen for him and almost... she had almost made love to him. Adrian, the murderer of young girls.

"Redlynn, wait." Adrian moved toward her.

"Don't! Don't touch me," she warned in a low voice, backing away further still.

"If you'd let me explain," he begged.

"Explain what? Explain how you let these... these... creatures of the devil steal and murder children? *Children*, Adrian! No more." Redlynn looked over the room. "I am Redlynn Mactire Fola, of the Sisterhood of Red, and I will not let this continue. I will do what none of you have seen fit to do. I will go out and find the rest of the girls, if there are any, and kill the Were king."

A dumbstruck look came over Adrian and Blain's faces. Neither man moved as she ushered Lizzy up the stairs and out of sight. When she reached his room, she slammed the door behind her and pushed the bar across.

Redlynn rushed to the window and inhaled deeply. She had to get out of here. Involuntarily, she grasped for her locket, but it wasn't there. Redlynn looked down in her bodice; her necklace was gone. She spun on the spot, searching the floor, but found nothing. Where had she last seen it?

Lizzy cowered in the corner, pulling Redlynn from her search. She had to think more than just of herself right now.

Redlynn sucked in a deep breath, took Lizzy by the arm, marched her into the bathroom, poured water into the basin, and washed the dirt from her face, neck and hands.

"Tell me, Lizzy. Tell me everything."

CHAPTER FIFTEEN

"Find Angus," Adrian said to Blain in a low voice. "Now."

Blain nodded and immediately left the dining hall.

Was it possible Redlynn was the child of a wolf and a sister? It made sense, how could it be any other way? How had he not thought of it sooner?

"Lord Adrian." Hanna's small voice broke through his thoughts. "She'll come around. Were any of us any different when you first explained?"

Adrian watched the women; they stood, stoic and brave. Each had gone through what Redlynn was going through, and each had come out the other side, understanding the lies they'd been told by his mother and now Lillith, the Head of the Sisterhood. But this was different, because she was different.

He found it remarkable that Redlynn remembered anything from her shift the night before. He didn't remember his first dozen or more shifts. Even the next fifty were mostly a blur, but over the years his father had taught him how to control it, how to focus and remember in his human form what he did in his wolf form. In time, Redlynn would remember as well. Adrian had to tell her before it happened.

"Go to your mates and young," he told the women. "I'll take care of this."

"My sister," said Clara.

"I'll bring her to you as soon as I'm able. I promise."

"Thank you, M'lord."

As the women filed out, Blain retuned with Angus. His face was unreadable.

"Prince Adrian," said Angus. "You wanted to see me?"

"Your surname is Mactire Fola, is it not, Angus?"

"Aye, you know it is."

"Have you ever been with a female, Angus? A Sister?"

Angus eyed them both suspiciously. "Aye."

"How long ago?" asked Blain.

"Why do you ask?"

Adrian sat down and blew out a breath. "You've done nothing wrong, Angus, but this is important."

Angus sighed and sat down heavily on a wooden bench. He stared at the table for a long time without speaking. "She died a few winters back. She was the one. My mate. I met her close to twenty-five years ago while she gathered herbs in the woods. After a year of meeting in the woods, I told her what I was. Her mother was the Head of the Order, and she grew scared that the Sisterhood would find out about us."

Angus stopped speaking. He rubbed his fingertips together as if remembering the feel of something. The burden of grief that Angus had carried all these years was suddenly very apparent to Adrian. There'd always been a sadness to him, but Adrian had chalked it up to having lived so long and never finding a mate. He'd been wrong; Angus' sadness had been brought about because he had found his mate.

"Angus, have you seen Red?" Blain asked.

Angus shook his head. "No. I've heard of the new female, but I haven't seen her."

"We think she might be your daughter," said Adrian.

"Raeleen's daughter?" Angus' eyes widened.

"Her name is Redlynn Mactire Fola."

146

Angus smiled, lost in thought. "Explains the scent I caught on you a few days back. I thought it was just my imagination. I catch a whiff of Raeleen everywhere."

"Angus, we need your help," said Blain. "She's going to get herself hurt."

Watching Angus' pain made it clear to Adrian that losing Redlynn now would be worse than anything he'd endured. What he'd felt the night before in the woods was just the beginning of what he'd feel if she left for good. He had to make her see the truth.

"What do you need from me?" Angus stood. His shoulders squared, and Adrian watched the years fall from Angus' face. His eyes twinkled.

"She hasn't been told the truth about us yet. But it's complicated. Girls have gone missing from Volkzene in recent months. A wolf has betrayed our oath and given children to the Bloodsuckers. Redlynn is hell-bent on killing me because she thinks I'm responsible."

"Then we need to tell her." Angus looked between them.

"Yes, but..." Adrian trailed off.

"It's not that simple," said Blain. "She's the chosen one, the one from the prophecy."

"*My* daughter?" Angus's voice rose.

"That's not all," said Adrian. "Last night... Angus, last night she shifted."

Angus's mouth opened and closed several times before he spoke. "That's not–"

"Possible. Yes, we know. But we were there; it happened. We need you to talk to her with us. To help her understand we aren't the enemy."

"My daughter. My daughter is a she-wolf," Angus laughed, scratching his graying beard.

"She's my mate, Angus. Help me."

A sudden intensity came into Angus' face. "Och, aye. I'll help you, my king."

Adrian, Blain and Angus stood outside the door, staring at it. His heart pounded. This was the moment. It was so different than all the mates he'd explained the truth to before. Different because they hadn't been his woman. Or a wolf. Now, with his heart at stake, he was terrified.

"If she's anything like her mother, she ain't gettin' any softer in there," said Angus.

"She'll get through it. So will you. Together, you'll change our kingdom forever. Believe that." Blain knocked before he could protest.

He glared at Blain. There was no sound from inside. The hairs on his neck stood up, and his heartbeat quickened.

"Redlynn," he called, knocking.

Again, there was no answer.

Something was wrong. Adrian tried the handle; it was locked. He pounded on the wood.

"Redlynn! Open the door!" This was not the way to get her to comply, but the terrible gnawing in his gut grew.

He heard the shuffling of feet and breathing from the other side. Pressing his face to the crack, he inhaled deeply. It wasn't Redlynn's scent.

"Lizzy." He tried to control his rising panic. "Lizzy, open the door to my room, please." The wolf in Adrian's chest growled with impatience.

"Red... Red told me not to."

"Lizzy. Tell Redlynn that I need to talk to her."

"I... She's not here."

Adrian howled in rage. Angus grabbed him from behind as Adrian pounded his fists on the door.

The lock clicked and the bar moved. He didn't care what the girl saw when she peeked out at them, but it seemed to terrify her.

148

"Red went to find the other girls. I tried to stop her, honestly I did. She's strong, but even Red isn't strong enough to take on *all* the bloodsuckers."

"Close the door, lass," Angus said in a gruff voice. "Wait for the women ta come get ya."

Lizzy nodded and quickly slammed the door, locking it again.

"Adrian," Angus said. "Boy, look at me.

He was close to gone. His wolf so near the surface that he barely kept him at bay. The tremors had already begun; his nails were lengthening, and fur sprouted on his hands. He tried to focus on Angus' face.

"We'll get her back. I lost her mother, I'm not gonna lose her, too, and neither are you. If it takes my last breath."

Adrian nodded. The fear and anger building inside of him was going to explode any minute.

Blain took Adrian's face in his hands. "Go. Find her."

Adrian was down the hall in three strides. He shifted mid-air as he leapt from the balcony to the dining hall below. Men had flooded into the hall and watched as he landed on the main table on all fours. Turning, he faced his men. This was it. His time had come. The howl that emanated from his chest was like none he'd loosed before.

It was the call. The call of the king.

Within minutes, all men from the castle had assembled in the dining hall. Jale and Juda were the last to enter. Adrian howled again, so loud that the glass clattered in the window panes. Each man bent low to knee and bowed to their king, except for Jale and Juda, who continued to stand. If they continued to disobey, he'd have to fight them for control. Adrian didn't want to have to kill them in a fight to the death. Strength filled him, and determination. There was no going back now.

He pierced them with his gaze, and gave them one last chance, loosing a third call. Reluctantly, the brothers fell to their knees.

Adrian let his gaze rest on each of his men in turn. It is done. With the bowing of each man, his fate was sealed. He was now King of the Wolves. Adrian barked and leapt off the table, making for the exit. The sounds of clothes ripping and snarls erupted behind him as his men shifted. Dax stood waiting, watching the scene unfold.

At the gate within seconds, he sniffed the air and caught her scent easily. His men ran up behind him, followed by Dax's giant, white bear form.

"My mate is in the woods. She's in danger. Vampires have been stealing girls, and she has gone to save them. Find her. Help her. Keep her safe."

Blain and Angus flanked him as he tore off into the trees. Over rocks and branches, the three sprinted into the woods. They hadn't gone far when the rain started up again. Moisture clung to everything, dampening the earth and diluting her scent, making Redlynn's trail harder to track. For an hour or more, they spread out through the forest trying to find her.

"We've run the river," Roal said.

"I've checked the border to the farmlands," panted Fendrick.

"The clearing is empty of her scent," Law said.

"She has to be somewhere," Adrian growled to himself.

"Blain, Roal, Law, Paulo, to the north border. Patrol for vampires."

"Where now?" asked Angus.

Adrian stopped and sniffed the air. Where was she? Anxiety wracked him. He needed to find her and keep her safe. It was the only thing that mattered. How was it possible that he couldn't find her? He swore.

"What is it?" Angus asked.

"She's masked her trail somehow. That's why I can't smell her anymore." He whipped his head around in every direction. *"She could be anywhere."*

*****

150

Redlynn ran through the dim light into the woods with a speed she'd never experienced, and an exhilaration that thrilled her. Completely forgetting why she was there, she let herself run for a good twenty minutes before she heard the howls of the Weres. The sound stopped her mid-sprint. They were coming after her.

Back-tracking, she rushed to the tree where she'd left her bow and sword. Grabbing her red cloak, she lay it down in the wet leaves and dirt and stomped it into the ground, covering it in as much soil as possible before fastening it around her neck. Then she found stinkweed and rubbed it over her arms and legs. She swallowed the nausea that rose in her throat from the smell. Tossing the weeds aside, she slung her quiver and bow onto her shoulder, shoved her hunting knife into her boot, and pulled up her hood.

Her heart squeezed at the thought of Adrian. She still wasn't sure she was doing the right thing. Perhaps she'd been too rash. The look in his eyes as he'd pleaded with her to listen. She hadn't even given him the chance to explain. A howl sounded through the trees and her jaw clenched.

The Weres were close. She swung up high into a tree and waited. Weres passed far below her. First two or three, and then dozens, spreading out, searching for something. One stopped at the bottom of her tree and sniffed it. She held her breath as the brown Were circled. Her fingers twitched with the desire to loose an arrow on him. But the Weres were second on her list now. First, she had to find the other girls.

The Were was joined by a second brown Were, and Redlynn's heart thudded loudly. Lizzy had mentioned two brown Weres had taken her. The Weres raised their noses into the air and sniffed, looking up into the tree. Redlynn hid as close to the trunk as she was able. The first wolf lifted his leg and marked the tree. Then the two trotted off.

An urgency to find the ruins that Lizzy had mentioned became paramount. Redlynn jumped from the high branch and landed lightly below. That fever had certainly done something to her reflexes.

She located the moon, between a break in the cloud cover. A fat droplet hit her face. The sensation of brushing it away reminded her of when Adrian had done that very thing, just hours earlier. Her heart clenched at the knowledge that he'd lied to her. She thought she loved him, but how could she love someone who would allow such unspeakable things to go on around him, without doing anything about it.

Redlynn stifled a sob. She'd gotten so comfortable in Wolvenglen, feeling like she might actually belong there. Knowing now that she couldn't be with him meant that her only choices were to return to Volkzene, alone. Or move somewhere else all together. Her stomach churned at the thought of never feeling Adrian's strong arms around her again. She'd only known him for a few days, but the thought of not having him in her life now made everything else seem somehow worse.

Redlynn checked the sky again, waiting for the clouds to part. Clearing her mind, she tried to focus. She located north and headed in that direction. Being careful to avoid the Weres, she zigged and zagged through the brush, making her way across a clearing to a rock face Lizzy had remembered seeing. She stood in front of the rocks, memories flashing in her mind, images from her dream. She swallowed hard as a chill ran through her. She got the feeling her dream wasn't a dream.

From here, Lizzy had come from the west. Redlynn squinted at the night sky again. Rain drops pounded her body. She turned west, and an enormous white bear appeared out of the brush. She grabbed her sword and aimed it at the animal.

The bear didn't move. Its light hazel eyes seemed almost human. She'd seen bears before in the woods, but never a bear

152

with that color eyes before. Or an all-white bear. She needed to get him out of her path. Redlynn charged and the bear stepped back. She lunged at him, when a tall pale figure jumped from a rock and landed on the bear's back. The bear roared in anger, trying to shake the man off. Redlynn watched in horror as the man opened his mouth, exposing long deadly fangs. He plunged them deep into the bear's neck and the bear tumbled sideways. *Vampire.*

Redlynn froze on the spot. Using his nails, the vampire slashed and tore at the bear, opening gashes anywhere his fingers touched. An image of Lizzy lying in a dark ruin, being subject to those fangs and nails, set Redlynn aflame. She charged the vampire, unable to control her anger. She swung her sword. He leaned away and she missed him by inches. Blood dripped from his mouth, down his chin, and onto his chest. His eyes were dead-cold, as if they'd never known joy.

"Oh, my, you smell so much better than the bear." He ran his tongue over his lips and grinned widely. "What's that I smell on you? It's human, but not all the way."

What was he talking about? "Are the girls still alive?" Redlynn demanded.

"Oh, the little Sweetings are not too far off. But you shall never find them. They're ours now."

"Where are the Weres that helped you take the girls?" Redlynn yelled. "Are they in the caves to the north?" Her gaze traveled to the white bear. He struggled to his feet.

The vampire's grin fell. "In the caves? Of course not, silly girl."

"Then where are they?" she asked.

"That's easy. The Weres are–"

The bear rose from the ground and slammed into him, knocking him over. Momentarily stunned by the movement, the vampire lay sprawled on his stomach. The animal clamped down on the vampire's throat. The vampire flailed beneath his giant maw. Redlynn stepped out of the way. The vampire struggled, trying to twist himself out of the bear's grasp. The bear shook him like a toy doll, and then let go. He rolled onto his back and the bear bit down once more, ripping his throat out. Redlynn's mind went numb at the sight of the vampire turning to mist and disappearing. The bear stumbled to the ground, panting.

Redlynn stared at the spot where the vampire had disappeared. Her rapid breathing was only matched by her accelerated heart rate. Lizzy had told the truth, and Adrian had been right. The vampire had been the most terrifying thing she'd ever seen. Between his cold, dead eyes and the ruthless way he'd torn into the bear, he'd been worse than any human she'd ever seen.

Her gaze travelled to the bear. Slowly she walked forward and knelt beside it. He tracked her movements and whimpered softly. She reached out her hand and pressed it on his oozing neck. The wound looked bad. Her heart went out to the creature who'd just risked his life for hers. She wanted to do more for him at that moment, but she didn't know what to do. With guilt in her heart Redlynn leaned in close to the bear's ear and whispered, "Thank you, and… I'm sorry."

*****

Adrian and Angus tore through the woods. They'd been going in circles for the past thirty minutes.

"I've found her," Dax said.

"Where are you?" Adrian stopped abruptly.

"At the cliff, near the clearing."

"Don't hurt her."

"I'll try, but she's not looking too friendly."

"Dax, I give you permission to defend yourself if she attacks. But don't hurt her. And don't let her get away." Adrian turned and ran hard toward the spot where they'd picked up Lizzy the night before.

154

"She's covered in stinkweed." Dax's chuckle was cut short. "Wait–"

"Dax? Dax!"

"Bloodsuckers!" Dax roared.

Adrian snarled, coming to a halt. He needed to think. Everything was happening at once. Focus. "Everyone reinforce the borders until I get to her. Then we find the girls and end this."

"What about me?" asked Blain.

"You stay on patrol. Angus with me. Dax? Dax?"

There was no answer.

Adrian and Angus sprinted toward the rocks. He needed to find her.

CHAPTER SIXTEEN

The bear reached out with a large paw, opening a deep cut to Redlynn's arm, probably fearing for his life, forcing Redlynn to hit him in the head, knocking him out. "Sorry," she said. Redlynn stood over the unconscious body of the bear. She contemplated putting him out of his misery. Blood trickled down her arm.

Crap. A trail.

Redlynn tore a strip off the ever-shortening hem of her red cloak and tied it around her arm. *There's going to be nothing left to this darn thing if I don't stop getting injured.* Blood seeped through the makeshift bandage quickly. She had to get moving.

At a run, she headed west again. The woods crawled with Weres tonight, hunting her, but she hadn't seen one in quite some time. Something wasn't right. Maybe they were meeting with the vampires. She pushed the thoughts from her mind; it didn't matter, she had no time to think on it. The ruins where the girls were being held were on the west border of the Wolvenglen Forest, next to the Daemon Wastelands. She remembered the story Adrian had told her earlier about the djinn.

Rumors of the Wastelands and the monsters that inhabited them were enough that the Sisterhood was forbidden to enter them. Crafty. If the vampires knew anything about the Sisterhood, they'd know that this was the perfect hiding spot for the stolen girls.

Climbing a rock, she emerged on an outcropping. It overlooked the forest below. She saw where the red and green tree line ended, and the black, scorched earth of the Wasteland began. She'd never actually seen the Wastelands before, and the very sight of them left her with a feeling of dread. Right on the edge of the wood before the beginning of the barren landscape, Redlynn spotted a group of crumbling buildings. *The ruins.*

Her foot slipped on the wet rock, and Redlynn pitched forward violently. Her mind grew dizzy at the thought of falling. She blew out a long, low breath, trying to quash the rising panic inside her. She'd never been fond of heights.

Throwing off her hood, she lifted her face to the heavens, letting the rain fall on her, trying to calm her shaky nerves. The reality of her situation slapped her. She was but one woman, alone in the woods, being chased by Weres, going off to rescue a group of girls, while killing a horde of untold numbers of vampires. The image of the blood-soaked vampire ripping into the flesh of the white bear flashed through her mind.

What has my stubbornness done to me this time? Most likely it's gotten me killed. She took another deep breath. A new scent hit her.

Adrian. She peered into the rain-drenched woods. Two Weres emerged from the trees onto the large rock outcropping where she stood exposed, still on the edge. The huge, black Were with golden eyes that she'd seen before, and an equally massive wolf with a shock of red fur stared at her. Redlynn's breath caught. She recognized the red Were. She'd remember him for as long as she lived. He'd been the one that chased off her father when she was young. And the black wolf was from the gate and her dream. He was the king.

Anger ripped through her at the sight of the two Weres. She drew her sword and prepared for battle. She wasn't going to let either of them get away. The king moved forward till he was only a

157

few yards away. She steadied her breathing and stepped forward to attack. Suddenly the air around the king shook and his body twitched and convulsed. His feet shortened and his legs lengthened. Redlynn's jaw dropped and her sword hand went slack. The black hair on his body receded and his spine straightened. Redlynn's mouth dried. Within a minute he stood, a naked man before her. And when he lifted his face, her heart sank.

"No," she whispered, her voice cracking.

"Redlynn." Adrian held his hand out to her.

"Not you. It can't be you," she screamed. *How could it be him? This whole time. First the sisters, now Adrian. How was I so stupid as to trust any of them?* "Weres are beasts." She shook her head.

"Let me explain."

Her mind was on overload. The Weres were shape-shifting men. "You knew why I was in the woods. You knew I was hunting you. You led me on."

"Redlynn, you have to believe me now, I don't know who took the girls." He took another step toward her. "I'm trying to find out. But right now, we're not safe; you need to come with me. There are—"

For the first time, she saw him for what he was. She took a deep breath. "You're the king of the Weres."

"Wolves," Adrian corrected, standing straighter. "Yes, I am the King of the Wolves."

How was this possible? How had she fallen for him? He was her enemy. The one she'd left the Sisterhood to kill. Instead, she'd fallen in love with him. Like Hanna and Clara and all the others. She'd fallen for a Were.

"You lied to me," she said through gritted teeth. Her eyes narrowed. "I trusted you."

"You feel it in your heart, Redlynn, I know you do. We were meant for each other. You are my mate. My queen."

Her mother's words flooded her. "*Someday you will be a queen.*"

"No." Redlynn shook her head and raised her sword. "Not this, not this way."

"You *know* it's the truth. Last night, the fever, that wasn't an infection. It was your wolf, fighting inside you to be released."

What was he talking about? She was a Sister, a werewolf hunter. This isn't possible. It can't be true. "It was just a fever."

Her gaze swept across Adrian's naked body, and something stirred at the sight of him. Images of him in the river, and on a bed of moss, flashed into her mind. Dreams? Memories?

The memory of his skin on hers under the moonlight made her heart want nothing more than to run to him. But he betrayed her trust. He'd lied.

Acid roiled in her stomach. She needed to get away. She needed to think. But this wasn't the time. The girls needed her. Like a rope wound too tight, one more thing and she'd snap.

Adrian motioned to the red wolf behind him. The wolf moved to stand directly behind him and shifted into human form. "I need for you to meet someone."

All she saw was his face over the top of Adrian's shoulders, but she recognized it immediately. He had flame hair and a red scraggly beard.

"This is Angus," Adrian said. "Your father."

Memories bombarded Redlynn of the night her father had fled from Volkzene. Redlynn had snuck from where her mother had hidden her, back to the house, to find her father drunk and in a rage. Her mother arrived a short time later with a man with red hair. Her mother hadn't seen Redlynn.

Watching through the kitchen window, Redlynn witnessed the red-haired man confront her father. He'd grabbed a knife and threatened to kill them all. There was a scuffle and a ferocious red-furred Were had appeared out of nowhere, the first she'd ever seen.

It had attacked her father, but her mother had gotten in between them, stopping the Were. Wounded, her father had limped off into the night, never to be seen again.

Redlynn's breathing quickened and she blinked rapidly. The Were from that night was Angus. But that didn't make him her father. Her father had been a human, and Angus had driven him off.

"You remember me, lass? Your mother–"

"You drove off my father."

"No." Angus shook his heavy head. "I'm yer father. That human was yer step-father."

"I saw you almost kill him, through a crack in the hut wall."

"Aye. I did. But I did it for Raeleen and for you. He was a drunkard and a fiend. I did it to protect both of ya."

Redlynn hit her forehead with the flat of her sword. This couldn't be true. Memories from the night before flooded her. The pain, the breaking of the bones, rolling in the grass.

"No!" she shouted. She didn't want to be this. She was one of them. Everything she'd been taught to fear and hate. It wasn't possible. Her mother would've told her if it were true. Her heart sank. She didn't know who to believe anymore.

Adrian moved closer.

She stepped away. "Don't come near me! It isn't true. I'm not a Werewolf. I'm not!" She backed up. Her foot slipped, and she couldn't find traction. She looked up to see the terror on Adrian's face as he sprinted forward. The soil beneath her fell away.

The ground below rushed up to meet her, making her stomach lurch from the drop. Adrian and Angus yelled her name from above. Time seemed to slow as she plummeted through space. Looking to the sloping ground below, Redlynn's thoughts were of her death.

She hit the muddy ground with a thud and rolled down the hill. A rock struck her temple and she lost hold of her mud-slicked sword, continuing downward without it. Leaves and brush tangled in her cloak, scratching at her legs. Redlynn cried out as she slammed into the trunk of a large redwood, and the air rushed out of her. Her muscles clenched and every inch of her body screamed in pain. She stood, trying to breathe. Her legs wobbled, and she leaned on the wet tree for support. Bending at the waist, she gulped in air and tensed, waiting to see what hurt the most.

A cry escaped her and she raised her hand to her mouth. Nothing in her life was what it seemed. She wished she'd never left Volkzene.

Weres howled on the cliff-top above her, pulling her from her thoughts. She scanned the surrounding area for her sword. It was nowhere to be seen. All she had now was her bow and knife. They weren't much, but at least she was a great shot.

Reality settled in again. She needed to move. She was stunned and injured, but Adrian and Angus would be close behind. Now was not the time to think. The girls needed her. She'd figure things out with Adrian and her new-found life later.

She sped down the rest of the incline till she hit level ground again.

*****

Adrian watched in horror as one moment Redlynn stood before him, and the next she was gone. Running to the edge of the cliff, he peered over the unstable edge. Trees and rocks jutted from the earth. All things she could be impaled on or struck by. Angus grabbed him by the arm, and hauled him back.

"That's not the way to get her. We need to go down the side." Angus pulled on him.

"She hates me, Angus."

"No. She's confused and hurt, but she knows the truth."

"Is that enough?" Adrian's chest constricted. "My mother knew the truth. She knew that my father had been magicked into sleeping with another. It didn't make her stay."

161

Angus slapped Adrian's cheek lightly. "Stop it. Redlynn isn't Irina. Ya need to let go of the past, boy. It's the only way you'll have a future."

The slap cleared Adrian's head. He heard a howl in the distance. She was out there, possibly dying. He needed to get to her. Adrian shifted and howled, muzzle to the sky. "*She's at the west border. Angus and I are going after her. Paulo, go to the rocks near the clearing. Bo, go with him, find Dax and make sure he is still alive. Blain, grab a dozen men and meet me at the western border. Everyone else be on the lookout for vampires. Kill on sight.*"

Adrian followed Angus, and the two lumbered down the side of the mountain, too slow for Adrian's liking. *What if she were hurt? Or bleeding? Or dead?* With vampires in the woods, they could find her first. He shuddered at the thought. And knowing her strength of will, there was no way she wasn't already moving forward.

Half-way down, he hooked a left and found an imprint where she'd hit the ground. He continued westward. Within minutes he found her sword, discarded in the mud. Dashing past it, he continued down the hillside. He stopped at a tree smeared with blood. Sniffing at it, he whimpered. It was hers. If it were from a leg wound, he might stand a chance of catching up to her.

"*Get her scent,*" Adrian ordered Angus.

"*I already know it.*"

"*Let's find her before she gets herself killed.*"

The two wolves sped off into the damp night.

*****

Redlynn made her way across the valley, heading to the border. The closer she got, the more ominous the landscape became. Before long there were no more animals. No birds squawked, no squirrels hunkered in hollows. There was nothing but the sound of the rising wind as it whistled through the

162

Wasteland. The air grew thick and heavy with the smell of acrid smoke. She stopped, taking several deep breaths to acclimate to the air. The clouds above the trees blanketed the sky, making the evening oppressive. A howl sounded far behind her, making her respite short-lived.

What the hell am I doing? Redlynn thought. *I should wait.* Wait for whom? Adrian? Her heart squeezed and took in a shuddered breath. She loved him. But how could she be what she'd been taught to hate? Her mother had, though. All those years when she'd found her mother crying. Her mother had said that she missed Redlynn's father. Redlynn had always assumed her mother missed the man that had raised Redlynn. And the times she'd tried to talk to her mother about what she'd seen, her mother had shushed her and told her never to speak of the Weres.

A rustle in the trees pulled Redlynn from her thoughts, and she scanned the valley forest surrounding her. She couldn't see any movement, but a chill of cold breath ran over her neck. Whipping around, she found a pair of pale, blue eyes framed by the palest face she'd ever seen, completely drained of color. Redlynn backed up quickly from shock. He was handsome, with full red lips and long, blond hair.

"Hello." His smile made a shiver run down her spine.

Redlynn pulled her bow and notched an arrow.

"I don't want to hurt you." He held up his hands. "I'm assuming you are looking for the girls of the Sisterhood."

"Who are you?"

"My name is Sage. If you follow me, I can take you to them."

Redlynn's heart thundered. "Why? You're a vampire."

"Don't judge. Not all vampires are equal, just as not all Weres are equal, as I am sure you know." Sage gave her a knowing smile.

Redlynn didn't answer. She and the vampire circled, assessing each other. He looked so different from the one that had attacked her. He was dressed nice, and spoke with a dignified air. His eyes sparkled with humor.

"You should hurry." Sage pointed in the direction of the ruins. "Both the vampires and the Weres will converge soon."

That meant the vampires weren't there yet. She still stood a chance of getting there before them, and getting the girls to safety.

The vampire's nostrils flared and he frowned. "You smell different."

"I bet," Redlynn mused.

"Try to keep up." Sage smiled and took off toward the west.

He moved with a speed so quick that Redlynn was sure he simply would've vanished from sight before her shift.

Wait... *my shift?* The memory of howling at the moon flooded back to her. *No! I am not a Were.* She put her bow away and raced after him. Keeping up proved easier than it should have. She smiled, running neck-and-neck with him. Her stride and balance compensated easily on the dead, metallic loam as they left the trees and moved into the Wastelands. Rocks jutted from the ground like black spires from hell. They slowed until Sage stopped and made his movements more deliberate.

"I knew you were different." His smile broadened.

When they reached a large clump of tightly clustered rocks, Sage stopped and pointed. Redlynn followed his finger, spotting the large stone ruins. He gently took her chin and turned her face to the right. He pointed to a stone doorway with a broken gate and a fallen stone angel lying nearby. It looked like a crypt, with stone steps descending underground.

"There," he whispered, stepping closer to her. "You might find that structure of interest."

Redlynn peered at the area and breathed deeply. A foul stench reached her nose over the scents of the rain. Sage's cool fingers slid down her throat and rested on her pulse. The sensation gave Redlynn the chills. Slowly she turned to face him, and noticed his

164

eyes locked on her throat. Lifting her leg, she pulled her hunting knife from her boot and pressed it to his stomach. His nostrils flared and his smile tightened. His gaze flicked to the wound on her arm, from where the white bear had gashed her. Redlynn yanked the bloodied strip from her arm and tossed it to the ground. The flesh underneath was already closed.

"Don't worry, Love. I don't drink Were."

Her eyes narrowed and adrenaline coursed through her. "Back. Up."

Quick as light, he grasped her wrist and lifted it to his heart, making her gasp. "If you're going to stick a vampire, you need to aim higher than that. The heart will stun, the throat is a kill. Anything else will just piss us off."

"I'll remember that." She tried to keep her voice from shaking.

"You go. I'll keep watch."

This had to be a trap. Her gaze travelled to the crypt entrance again and back to Sage. "Why are you helping me?"

"Because..." Sage's voice faltered. "Because I have done terrible things in the name of being a vampire, and I want to try and make amends."

Redlynn wondered why she trusted this unknown man when she wouldn't even trust Adrian. It was something about his eyes; behind the bravado, he looked completely lost. And desperately hungry. He was starving. Redlynn had seen the signs of starvation all too well.

"You better hurry, She-Were," he said.

Redlynn nodded, removed her knife from where the tip pressed against his heart, and tucked the blade into her boot. She readied her bow, her heart pounding in her chest. She stepped into the open, trained her bow, and slowly made her way around fallen ruins toward the crypt entrance. The rain slowed and she sniffed the air; the heady smell of ash permeated the area. Creeping closer to the stairs, she kept herself alert to her surroundings.

Redlynn arrived at the metal doors, bent and broken. The foul stench that wafted up from the crypt overpowered her senses: a mix of stale air, blood and feces. The sound of moving chain reverberated from somewhere in the dark down below. She moved with trepidation; water rolled down the stairs under her feet. She tried to keep her breathing quiet and even to minimize the tremors that ran through her body. Dread filled her at the thought of what she might find.

The lower she descended, the darker it became. Even with her improved eyesight, it was difficult for her to see beyond the stairwell. A moan floated up, along with a light cough. Redlynn reached the last step, and slipped on a piece of damp moss. Her ankle twisted and she hit the floor with a clatter. Sharp pain shot up her leg as it twisted at an odd angle, and she landed sideways and dropped her bow in an effort to stop the fall. So much for the element of surprise.

Sitting on the floor in the dark, she heard whimpers. It took several seconds for her vision to adjust. She wrinkled her nose at the smell that lingered in the small chamber. Blinking rapidly, her vision adjusted. All along one wall, girls of the Sisterhood were chained to the stone. Some were limp, their heads lolled to the side, possibly dead already. Others sat staring blankly into the darkness. She was too late.

A girl turned, her dirty gown caked in dried blood smears, blinking several times as if she couldn't comprehend what she saw.

"Red?" she whispered. The girl couldn't focus fully. "Red? Is that Red?"

It was Sasha, the Cantrel's daughter. She hadn't been gone more than a week, but she looked as pale and dirty as the rest.

"Red," another whispered. "You came."

One by one the girls roused, their glassy eyes trying to focus on her. Redlynn moved toward the first girl. Her chest squeezed as she reached her. It was Yanti. Redlynn's ankle twinged as she put her weight on it.

Yanti crawled toward her. "Red."

"It's me. I'm here." She scooped the girl up in her arms. "How did you get here?"

Yanti squeezed Red tightly. "I was taken two nights after you left."

Tears threatened to spill, but she had to keep her wits about her. She scanned the crypt. The wall opposite bore floor-to-ceiling shelves of skulls. Human and non-human. Large, dust-covered urns perched on pedestals in the corners. Water seeped through the crumbling blocks, throwing moisture into the air.

"Red, help us." Yanti's long wrist chains scraped on the floor.

"Hush. Let me see your shackles."

Yanti lifted her arm. Bite marks marred the pale, soft flesh of the young girl. The sight made Redlynn want to scream. How could anyone do this? She pulled at Yanti's heavy, iron shackle, but it was fastened tight. Her fingers trailed the chain to the wall. The stone surrounding the peg crumbled. Pressing her feet into the wall on either side of the chain, Redlynn pulled. Her ankle no longer pained her, but the chain was fastened tight.

"Here, turn around," she said

Yanti turned her body and faced the wall. She put the girl in her lap.

"When I tell you to, pull." Redlynn took a deep breath. "Pull."

Yanti grasped the chain and the two of them leaned back as far as they could. There was a screech of metal and the wall gave way. The bolt pulled loose and landed with a loud clank. Yanti smiled and threw her arms around Redlynn.

"Thank you, Red. Thank you."

Voices outside floated down the stairs, and a chill ran through her.

"Help me get everyone out of here."

A shadow crossed the entrance to the crypt. Two bodies moved speedily down the stairs.

"They're coming," a girl cried.

Redlynn reached for her bow and notched an arrow. She pushed Yanti behind her, as she shuffled to the far wall. The girls whimpered and tried to cringe into the walls.

She pulled her bow string taut and didn't wait to see who it was before she loosed the arrow. The man in the front caught it mid-air.

"Good shot," came Blain's jovial voice.

"Blain!" Redlynn cried.

Sage stood behind Blain, in the shadow of the wall.

"Don't you have any clothing? These are children."

"Sorry," said Blain. "I don't usually keep my wardrobe stashed around these ruins."

"Honestly," she chastised, ripping off her cloak and throwing it at him.

Blain tossed her arrow to her. She shoved it in her quiver as he tied the cloak around his waist and through his legs. A ripple of disquiet travelled through her at the memory of Blain's betrayal.

Girls first, my problems later, she reminded herself. "The chains can be pulled from the wall. Help get the girls out."

The men worked quickly and pulled on the chains. Within minutes, the girls were freed.

"I'll go back up to keep watch." Sage dodged up the steps.

Weakly, the girls rose to their feet and the group moved up the steps, out into the open. Evening was upon them, but with the low clouds and the ash from the Wastelands, it looked like night had fallen. The girls breathed in deep lungfuls of the ashy night air as if they were in the grassland fields of the Westfall. Redlynn vaguely understood what they felt, having been shut up in the castle for days. But it wasn't the same.

Two men appeared from the trees. Redlynn's heart sank. It was the brothers Jale and Juda.

"Is Adrian with you?" Blain asked.

"No," said Juda.

The hairs on Redlynn's neck stood up. The way the brothers eyed the girls didn't feel right. "Blain, I think—"

But Redlynn's words were cut off by movement in the trees. The girls backed up toward the crypt entrance. She notched an arrow. A dozen tall pale men with lips like blood moved out of the shadows and surrounded the group.

"Well, what have we here?" asked the leader with a broad, pointy-toothed smile. "Runaways?"

"Let them go." Sage stepped beside her.

The leader's gaze narrowed on Sage. "Well, well, well. If it isn't my traitorous cousin, Prince Sageren, living in exile. Tell me, Sage, you're looking a bit worse for wear; how's that squirrel blood doing for you these days?"

"It's doing better for me than the rats you call gourmet, Garot."

Garot laughed, "Oh no, cousin. I have all I can eat, right here." He took in a long breath. "Mmmm. Fear. I love the blood of a fearful virgin. Oh! And what is that?" Garot inhaled again. "My, my. What is that new aroma? She is delectable. I'll sample her first. I've never had the blood of a half-breed before."

"I'd love to see you try." She pulled her bowstring tighter.

"You won't touch her," Blain snarled. His muscles twitched.

"Oh, but Blain, my dear boy, wasn't this what you wanted? Wasn't this our agreement? You bring me virgin blood and I don't slaughter you."

"What?" Redlynn loosened her bowstring for a moment in surprise. It couldn't be true. *Blain? Not Blain. He'd... He'd what?*

169

What did she really know about him? Redlynn couldn't comprehend the betrayal. First Adrian, now Blain.

"Not her." Blain ignored her. "You can't have Redlynn. She's Adrian's."

Garot's eyes skittered over her with a newfound interest. "I like it. The princess, is she?"

"Adrian is king. He has become Alpha."

"A queen." Garot's fangs grew long and sharp. "Even better."

Redlynn's mind spun and her breathing quickened. Blain. All this time, it was Blain who'd been responsible for the kidnapped girls. Suddenly she wished with all her might that Adrian were there.

"Well, this chat has been lovely; we are quite hungry after our long trip from Tanah Darah, so I think we will get our meals and go. Feel free to scream, or run or both. We do like to work up an appetite." Garot laughed.

"This is your only warning. Let them go, or die."

Garot laughed. "Oh, Blain, you are so wrong." He motioned to his men. "You think you can just take them because you say so? That's not how this works, mutt. In fact, tonight, it's you who are going to die. And her." He pointed to Redlynn. "And then your king."

"Not us," said Juda. "We had a deal and we stick by it. We'll still deliver girls, like we promised."

"Of course," smiled Garot. "You two are free. As is Blain, if he steps aside."

Blain turned to Jale and Juda. "Don't do this. She's the one. She has the mark. I saw it just above her left breast. She will end this for us."

Redlynn's mouth fell open. Her birthmark. "When have you seen my breasts?" she gasped.

"Show them," Blain urged. "Show them the mark."

170

"The one from the prophesy? How wonderful." Garot clapped his hands together. "My father will be most pleased when I bring you to him."

"The hell you will!" Redlynn loosed an arrow. Garot stepped out of the way but it hit a vampire behind him, directly in the chest. The vampire fell to the ground.

Garot attacked Blain mid-shift and took him to the ground, as well. Sage ran at two more of the vampires. The girls began to scream and run in every direction.

"The crypt!" Redlynn yelled. "Sasha, Yanti, get them in the crypt!"

The girls didn't move. Terror filled their faces.

"I'll get you back out," she promised.

Yanti and Sasha nodded, gathering the girls and herded them to their prison.

Grabbing an arrow, Redlynn searched for Jale and Juda, the need for vengeance rising inside of her once more. She wished she had her sword to run them through.

They'd shifted and were running for a rocky hill, heading toward the forest. Setting her sight on one of them, she loosed an arrow. Her foot sank in the loam at the last second and she missed; it struck a rock, glancing off.

"Dammit!" She pulled another, but the brothers disappeared.

Cursing the uneven soil, Redlynn swung back to the fray. She shot the second arrow and downed a vampire, as he ran at Sage.

Garot and Blain fought with a fierceness that would've torn a normal human apart. Her ankle now bore weight, but still ached. She hobbled over to the crypt, covering the entrance. Her next arrow missed a vampire, but he spotted her and his face contorted with rage. The vampire ran straight for her. Redlynn pulled her hunting knife from her boot, still favoring her rapidly healing ankle, and prepared to engage.

He raced within mere feet of where she stood before Blain jumped on him, knocking him to the ground and tearing out his throat. The vampire gasped and choked as blood poured from the wound, before dissolving into mist. Redlynn and Blain locked eyes, and before she could react, Garot reached out with his long nails and ripped open a gaping wound on Blain's flank. Blain yelped in pain, and Redlynn charged Garot.

Something inside of her clicked. Anger surged deep within. She used it to work past the pain of her ankle, attacking with a ferociousness she didn't know she possessed. Knocking into the vampire, she pushed him to the ground with surprising ease, her knife finding a resting place in his abdomen.

"You bitch!" Garot howled. He used both hands to shove her off. She sailed through the air and landed hard on her back, knocking the wind out of her for the second time that day.

Blain guarded the crypt entrance, trying to fight off three vampires. To the left of him, the smile on Sage's face told her he was enjoying the fight he was engaged in. Redlynn caught her breath and tried to push to her feet, but Garot loomed over her and pulled her knife from his stomach.

"Forget my father. I'm going to enjoy eating you, Queen." Garot bared his fangs and pushed her face to the side, lowering his mouth to her neck.

An ear-splitting roar came from the left. A giant black blur knocked Garot away. Howling wolves echoed all around the ruins.

Adrian. Redlynn flooded with relief.

Turning his shaggy head, she met his golden eyes with her own. Garot fell on him and the two took off, Adrian snarling and snapping at Garot's throat. The wolves fought ferociously against the remaining vampires. Everyone moved so fast that it was hard for her to take it all in.

A couple of feet away, Blain bled heavily in several places.

Getting to her feet, she found her bow. Adrian had Garot by the throat, and the vampire was trying to gouge at his eyes. Angus moved up next to Redlynn and stood between her and the rest of the fighting. His warm, russet-colored body was so familiar; she must have played with him as a child. *All this time…*

Redlynn held the arrow against her cheek and tried to track Garot, to take the shot, but Adrian was all over him. There was no way to hit Garot without hitting Adrian. She swore under her breath and looked to Blain. A vampire had him pinned on the ground and slashed at him with razor sharp nails. Redlynn aimed and fired, but the arrow missed in his frenzied movements.

His head whipped up and he ran at her. Blain was on his feet and leapt at the vampire from behind, but the vampire pulled Blain off and swiped at him, opening Blain's throat.

Redlynn pulled an arrow and let it fly. The vampire turned at the exact moment and the arrow caught him in the neck. He looked down in shock and then dissolved into mist.

Sage fought for his life, his movements so expert that he was a blur among the two vampires he battled. He kicked one in the face, forcing him toward a tree. Kicking him again in the chest, the vampire flew into the trunk, a broken branch sticking out of his chest. Sage pulled a sword from where it had been tucked at the small of his back and cut off the vampire's head.

The second vampire grabbed Sage from behind. Sage flipped him over onto his back and shoved his sharpened nails into the vampire's chest, ripping out the blackened heart. The vampire and his dripping heart dissolved the instant Sage beheaded him.

Redlynn turned to Adrian and found he'd shifted from his wolf form and held Garot in the air by his throat. Garot squirmed and kicked out like a babe. His long nails dug deep into Adrian's arms in an effort to get him to let go. Adrian's hard body was marred with cuts and abrasions, blood dribbling down his skin.

Deep gashes oozed on his back and side. Redlynn and Angus moved to where Adrian stood. Sage joined them.

"What do you think this will do, animal?" Garot choked. "Kill me; it won't change anything. My father will enact his revenge."

"Let him try," said Adrian. "Let all of them come. The prophecy is fulfilled. We will no longer hide in the forest. We will end the reign of bloodshed."

Garot choked, laughed, his breathing labored. His gaze drifted to Redlynn.

"He will betray you, she-Were. He will betray you the way his father betrayed his mother."

"My father," Adrian clenched his jaw, "was bewitched by a daemon."

"How stupid you dogs are. All it takes is the swish of a tail–"

Adrian roared in anger. Digging his claws into Garot's throat, he ripped open his larynx and dropped the vampire to the ground. Adrian raised his claws and prepared to administer the killing blow.

"No!" Sage grabbed Adrian's wrist. "Wait." Sage pushed aside his long leather traveling coat and pulled a knife out of a sheath strapped to his leg. It was a long, curved, white dagger, with a blood red stone in the hilt.

Garot laughed hoarsely. Air bubbled through the already closing hole in his throat. "And you, dear cousin," he croaked. "Your father was so gullible. Thinking that his court was loyal to his rule, when all along traitors lay all around him, waiting for the chance to strike"

"The only traitor was your father."

"Oh, cousin, how wrong you are."

Sage grabbed Garot by the hair and sliced off his head with one fluid movement. "For my father," he whispered.

Garot's body fell to the earth and his head stayed in Sage's grip. Sage mumbled a prayer that Redlynn couldn't decipher. The white knife glowed brightly and sucked in all of the blood that stained it. Then Sage sheathed it and stood.

"Good to see you again, King Adrian."

"And you, Prince Sage."

The men clasped forearms. The rain had turned to a light misting. Redlynn looked from the vampire's body, lying in the mud, his head in Sage's hand. "What kind of knife is that?" she asked.

"It is a Royal Blooded Cris. Blessed by the fae to kill a vampire, but preserve the body."

"What are you going to do with the body?" Adrian asked.

"Deliver it to the doorstep of my uncle."

"But won't he know it's you?" asked Redlynn.

"I hope so." Sage smiled.

Adrian turned to Redlynn. He had a cut across his chest that was healing already. He looked unsure of what to do. Angus moved out of the way, and Redlynn moved toward him. They stood staring at each other for several minutes, neither speaking.

"Where are the girls?" he asked finally.

"Over in the–" Redlynn broke off, glancing over her shoulder. Her gaze lit on the naked form of Blain on the ground. "Blain!" she yelled.

Dropping down on the soggy ground, she rolled Blain's head into her lap. Sage found the discarded scraps of Redlynn's cloak and covered him as much as possible.

"Blain." Adrian took his hand.

Blain's skin was slick with blood and sweat. Redlynn pressed her palm to his throat in an attempt to staunch the blood. Thick, warm liquid poured through her fingertips.

"Sorry... I didn't... see you... wield that sword." Blain gave her a shaky smile. His lips moved and he sucked in a bubbly breath. "Adrian. I'm sorry... It's been so long... I wanted to help… so you could rescue them… and take them home… show the Sisters the truth…"

Adrian nodded, but said nothing. Blain was responsible for the torture of these girls, but a part of her understood the need he had to protect his people. Wasn't that what she did, what she'd left her home to do? Wasn't she ready to kill the Weres, no matter the cost, to protect her village? He'd tried to save his race. But some things weren't worth the cost.

"You'll be fine, my brother," Adrian said. "You'll heal, and we can talk about it then."

Blain shook his head. "Not this time, I fear. Take her… she's the one…" Blain sputtered, coughed and choked, and then coughed some more. Bubbles of blood dribbled down his chin. His gaze locked on Redlynn's, and he sucked in one last, deep breath. "I'm sorry, golden sister, forgive…"

His eyes went glassy, and then blank. Redlynn chest squeezed, but no tears were shed. She reached down and kissed Blain on the forehead. Closing his eyes, she whispered, "I'll try."

CHAPTER SEVENTEEN

Adrian looked down at his best friend. How was it possible that Blain had done those things? To have stooped so low as to trust the vampires, and allow Sisters to be sacrificed. And for what? So they could fake a rescue and play the heroes by taking them home? Adrian stared into the face of the man he'd stood with as brothers, no longer even knowing who the man was.

Guilt wracked him, knowing that it was partly his fault this had happened. If he'd tried to go to the Sisterhood earlier, none of this would've happened. His men wouldn't be forced to gain physical affection from bought human women, and Blain wouldn't have resorted to doing the unthinkable. The betrayal at that moment went deeper than when his mother had left. *Probably how Redlynn feels about me.*

Sniffles and crying tore Adrian's thoughts from his friend. The girls re-emerged from the crypt.

"Girls," Redlynn called, standing. "These are the wolves of Wolvenglen. You were taken by wolves, but you need to listen to me when I tell you, these wolves will not harm you. We're going to take you with us, to Wolvenglen, and then in a couple of days, when you're well, I'll return you home."

Adrian's soul hit a pit of despair at her words. She was taking the girls back to Volkzene.

Trepidation showed all over the girls' faces.

"I won't let anything happen to you," Redlynn promised. The confidence and gentleness in Redlynn's voice tore at his heart. This was who she was meant to become. This was her destiny. To lead the Sisterhood.

The men shifted into wolf form, hiding their nakedness, and lumbered into the trees. Sage removed his coat and offered it to Adrian.

"Thank you." He rose and pulled it around his naked body.

"We'll see each other again soon, Adrian, King of the Wolves."

"You can count on it." Adrian extended his hand. "What will you do now?"

Sage shrugged. "Continue on. Watch and wait for the signs for the next prophecy. I want to regain my kingdom, but not at the cost of the lives of my friends. So I'll be patient."

"You are welcome to safe passage in my woods, whenever you find yourself in need."

"Thank you."

"I'll keep my promise, the wolves will stand with you."

Sage nodded. "With your new queen at your side, I hope the Sisters will return to you, and your people will once again be fruitful."

Adrian's gaze moved uncertainly to where Redlynn spoke to the girls. "I'm not so sure she is my queen."

"She is," Sage assured him.

He wanted to believe Sage's words. But Adrian had known a woman as stubborn as Redlynn before, and she'd never changed her mind.

"What did you mean when you said the next prophecy?" he asked.

Sage's brow furrowed. "Surely you didn't think there was just one prophecy pertaining to the whole of Fairelle?" Sage said. "The prophecy of the Sisterhood was the first to be recorded in the mage books. With that prophecy fulfilled, it opens the way for the others, beginning the reuniting of the lands. The bloodshed won't end until all have been fulfilled. When they are, then will we all finally find peace."

"I have a feeling that peace will be fought for, more than it will be found," said Adrian.

"You are most likely right." Sage stretched out his hand again. "May the blood of the vampires never soil your ground."

Adrian was surprised. Words of peace hadn't been spoken between vampires and wolves in hundreds of years. "And may the claws of the wolf never draw that blood," Adrian replied, grasping Sage's arm in a clasp of brotherhood.

The two men shook heavily, then parted. Sage disappeared with Garot's corpse into the trees.

*****

The group of Redlynn, Adrian, the wolves, and girls reached the castle by sundown. The girls were as shocked to see it as she'd been the first time. There were whispers about how it had gotten there, and how long it had taken to build.

Word spread quickly that they'd returned, and the women rushed out to meet them. Females hugged their husbands, children rushed up to their fathers, still in wolf form, and clung to them. The sight stirred Redlynn's heart. Such tenderness between the werewolves and their families broke down the walls of her heart. The girls watched the scene, wide-eyed and confused.

The women and children ushered the beleaguered group of girls inside, where everyone had injuries tended to, was bathed, fed, and put to bed for the night. Lizzy had made peace with the fact that her sister was alive, and she clung to her, to the great happiness of Clara. When the girls were in bed, Adrian and the men left to bury Blain in an ancient wolf burial ground. He hadn't spoken a word to her on the return journey, leaving her more confused than ever. For an hour, she stayed up and sat silently in the dining hall, alone in her thoughts. Finally, with nowhere else to go, she retired to Adrian's room to await his return.

Adrian didn't come back that night. In his absence, Redlynn spent hours in his bed, breathing in his scent and replaying all that had transpired between them. He'd never, technically lied to her. He'd just not been forthcoming with the truth of who he was. His words about the wolves had been weighted, neutral. He'd tried to protect her and keep her safe, even from herself. Though she didn't agree with how he'd gone about it, she understood.

The hours dragged on and the bed grew colder. Alone, her heart ached for his comforting touch. And she wished to comfort him in return. To soothe him in his pain, and ease his burden.

At first light, she awoke and went in search of him. The other men returned, but he was nowhere to be found. She came across Angus, eating in the dining hall. She hesitated momentarily. She'd come to terms with the fact that her dream was in fact, reality, but still had a hard time with him being her real father. Pulling up a chair, she sat with him.

"Have you seen Adrian?" She poured a mug of ale and downed it quickly, not meeting his eye.

Angus smiled warmly, put down his fork, and wiped his mouth. "He should be back soon, lass. He's grieving the loss of his friend."

Redlynn nodded. When Anya died, what had she done? She'd run out into the woods in an effort to kill the pain. But with Blain, there was no one to kill, no one to blame but the dead.

"You loved my mother."

"Very much." After a thoughtful pause, Angus added, "She was my mate."

"Why didn't she stay here?" She blurted it out, and then sucked in a deep breath.

Angus was quiet for a very long time, staring at his stew. "Your mother believed in tradition, in the Sisterhood. She believed that if she stayed with them, she'd change their minds about what they'd been taught. She believed she could fulfill the prophesy so we could be together."

"But she never did."

"No," Angus smiled sadly. "But you will." He stared at her. "You look so much like her. She'd be so proud of you."

Redlynn's throat tightened. "I don't know about that." Redlynn fixed her gaze on her intertwined hands. She filled her mug again. "I don't even understand what to tell them."

"Adrian's mother, Irina, was the High Sister of the Sisterhood of Red. When his father broke their mating vows and laid with another, she took all the females and left our woods. She vowed that never again would a Sister of Red be mated to a wolf, that wolves could not be trusted. From that day forward, all wolves were to be hunted and killed.

"But he was magicked into sleeping with someone else."

"Aye. But the queen didn't care. The king, overcome with grief, vowed that for his penance, we wolves would be bound to protect the Sisterhood from the vampires. Your mother betrayed the Sisterhood when she mated with me. Your grandmother forced her to marry a human, your step-father, to hide the shame."

"Did my grandmother know the truth?"

"I don't know. But she did know about your step-father's hobby of hitting women."

Redlynn's thoughts turned to Lillith. The way she'd always treated Redlynn and her mother, and the fact that she'd insisted Redlynn stay out of the woods. Something wasn't right. "Do wolves only mate with members of The Sisterhood?"

"The Sisters are the only ones able to bear wolf young. It goes back to the beginning. When Prince Garth made his wish with the djinn, Garth's wife, Princess Redlynn, was the first in the

181

Sisterhood of Red, which is why it was so named. She was a priestess of the Order of Mages at the time. She and the mages cast a spell on all of the mates of wolves, so that they'd be able to live longer and bear our young."

"So there were she-wolves, then?"

"No. The magick of the mages has been carried through the Sisterhood bloodlines, passing from mother to daughter. But in all this time, our daughters have never turned, just our sons. You're the first female Were. The first *ever*."

Redlynn studied the wooden table's surface for a long time without speaking. Angus sat silently, waiting, letting her think. Her thoughts were lost in the history of her people. How could they have been led so astray?

"There haven't been Sisters in Wolvenglen for close to a hundred years."

"No, there haven't. Not until recent years. Your mother was the first to come into the woods."

"And Hanna, Clara and the others? I'd been told that they'd moved south."

"Each of them came into the woods, just as you did. They ventured too far from the path and were led here."

Her mind tried to understand what Angus told her. "So, how is it possible that the wolves have survived? With no females and no young?" Angus stayed quiet till Redlynn worked it out. "How old are you?"

"Too old. We wolves can live to be two hundred, if the conditions are right."

Two hundred? Redlynn remembered the stories of Sisters in times past that would live to be a hundred and beyond. "The Sisters don't live past seventy."

Angus shook his head. "They don't anymore, but they used to. The magick that allows Sisters to carry our young, also connects our life forces, strengthening them to live longer."

Would she live to be two hundred? If she had daughters, would they?

"Why me?" she finally asked.

"Why not you? It was bound to happen at some point, given the prophecy."

"But I don't want to be the one," she said, almost to herself.

"That is something, daughter, that you will need to decide," said Angus.

Redlynn's heart clenched. No one but her mother had called her 'daughter' before.

"What?"

"Nothing." She stood.

Redlynn looked at the doorway. Adrian was out there, somewhere in the woods, grieving and in pain. Maybe she could let it all go, be who they all wanted and needed her to be. She could track him, find him.

A cry broke through her reverie. A girl ran into the dining hall, straight to Redlynn. The girl looked around wildly, apparently delirious. Redlynn pulled her close. Tears streamed down her cheeks as she clung to Redlynn.

Hanna and Lizzy rushed into the hall after her.

"I'm sorry," Hanna said. "She's dehydrated terribly. I went to feed the baby and when I returned, she'd gone from her bed."

"It's alright." Redlynn stroked the girl's hair.

"Ilsa." Lizzy walked to Redlynn's side and laid her hands gently on the girl's shoulders. "Ilsa, it's Lizzy."

Ilsa lifted her head, "Lizzy? Where are we?"

"We're safe, Ilsa. Come on, let's find you something to drink, and get you into bed."

Isla let go of Redlynn and clung to Lizzy instead. The girls needed another day to rest. None of them would truly recover until they were in the arms of their loving parents, though. She was going to have to take them home. And face the Sisterhood.

183

CHAPTER EIGHTEEN

Adrian stood outside his bedroom, knowing what was on the other side. The pain of Blain's betrayal had crippled him at the burial. Not wanting to see anyone, or allow Redlynn to see him so weak, he'd spent two nights in the solitude of his woods.

Emotionally and physically drained, he'd returned an hour ago and found the girls preparing to return to Volkzene. He'd spent thirty minutes working up the courage to face her, but now he stood, afraid to open the door. His heart couldn't handle hearing her say that she wouldn't be returning to him.

He'd seen how the girls needed her on the trek from the ruins. The way they looked to her for guidance, and protection. The prophecy was being fulfilled before his very eyes. She'd succeed with the Sisterhood, and they'd return to his wolves. His people would thrive again. He reminded himself that was what he'd always wanted. But for them... He'd betrayed her, lied to her. He'd done to her what he'd never wanted to do. And now she was leaving.

Taking a deep breath, he raised his hand to knock, and the door opened from within. Redlynn looked out at him, her eyes widened.

"Hi," he said.

She cleared her throat. "Hello."

She had her bow, quiver and bag already loaded.

"I'm taking the girls home today." She fidgeted with her bow string.

"I heard," he nodded. He wanted nothing more than to rush to her and hold her in his arms, to feel that she was all right and unmarred by the vampires, to have her console him in his grief over his friend. But he didn't. He wondered if it would have turned out differently if he'd been honest with her from the beginning.

He grasped for something to say. "Did you have any problems with anything, these last few days?"

She moved out of the doorway, and looked about the room. Finally she walked to the bed and straightened the already perfect duvet. "No. No problems."

His heart ached as he watched her, sure that he wouldn't see her for a long time, if ever. He couldn't stand the uncomfortable silence and unspoken words between them. Taking several strides toward her, he closed the distance between them. She turned and let out a small gasp at his nearness. He touched her cheek and breathed her fresh scent into his lungs.

He'd been a fool. He should've come to her instead of staying out in the woods for the last two days. He should have taken her into his arms and claimed her. He should have spoken words of endearment and love, telling her what he felt.

Adrian leaned in and pressed a light kiss on her mouth. She responded to his touch, pulling him closer to her. He wrapped her in his arms, allowing her to lead. Stroke for stroke her mouth heated on his, but just as soon as it started, she pulled away.

"Redlynn." He held her close. "Don't do this. Don't go." She was silent as she held onto him. He leaned away and tilted her chin, forcing her to meet his gaze.

"I need to finish what my mother began. I need to make the Sisterhood understand."

Adrian's heart sank as he took in her beautiful golden eyes. He nodded. "Do you want me to come with you?"

185

"Angus is going to see us to the village border."

At least his time away seemed to have helped her relationship with her father. "I understand." He backed away.

"Adrian." She reached for him.

"No. I understand, really, I do," he assured her. "You take them back safely. I'll be here if you need me."

Redlynn's brows knit in confusion, but then her face went blank. "We'll talk when I return."

Adrian nodded, but said nothing. Redlynn kissed him softly on the cheek and then stepped toward the door.

"Wait." He grabbed her hand and then quickly let go. "I found this for you. I thought you'd want it." He reached into his tunic and pulled her locket off his neck, holding it out to her.

"Thank you." She slipped it on and clutched the locket, pressing it to her breast.

At least I could bring her that piece of happiness. Adrian nodded, and then turned to the fireplace. He couldn't watch her leave. His wolf whimpered and cried out for her with longing. It had to be her decision. She had to decide her destiny; he couldn't decide it for her.

She walked out without another word, and Adrian stared up at the portrait of his mother. Hate soured his stomach, and bile rose in his throat at the sight of her. His father had betrayed her, but with her choice, to take the women and leave, she'd betrayed them all.

*****

Redlynn trudged through the woods with Angus and the rescued girls, confused by Adrian's actions. The last days without him as he mourned his friend in solitude had been agonizing. She understood his need to be alone, but his having let her go so easily was less well understood. She'd come to terms with what he'd done and why. And unlike with Blain, she'd forgiven him. But it seemed almost as if he'd been telling her goodbye. Like he didn't want her to return, though she was sure he did. At least, she

186

thought he did. Redlynn stopped walking. What if he'd changed his mind? Had her running from him turned his heart from her?

A hollowness filled her with dread. Agonizingly, she forced her feet to keep trudging forward, away from the castle and toward Volkzene, though every part of her wanted to fly to him and feel his strong arms around her. Something stirred inside of her, and she stopped moving and clutching her heart. Something moved inside, a being that was not herself. The being squirmed, itching to be let out.

"What's wrong?" Yanti stopped.

Redlynn couldn't articulate it in words. Her chest burned and her skin prickled as a tremor skittered over her body. She sucked in air, becoming overwhelmed with the need to get to Adrian.

"What's the matter, lass?" Angus moved to her side.

"I don't know," Yanti answered. "I think she's sick."

The blood pumped in her ears. A gut-wrenching pain twisted inside her, and she cried out.

"Redlynn!" Angus' voice was sharp as a knife.

All around, murmurs of the frightened girls floated around her.

"Lizzy!" Angus called. "Keep the girls moving. Redlynn just has a cramp. We'll catch up in a minute."

"Is she okay?" Yanti's voice trembled.

"Och, aye. She's fine. She just needs to relax for a moment. Redlynn, look at me, daughter." Angus' voice held a gentle but firm quality.

She tried to concentrate on Angus, as another tremor wracked her. Something inside fought to get loose.

"You feel her, don't you, your she-wolf? She's trying to get out, lass. You can't allow that. We have to get the girls to safety. I need you to find your she-wolf, dominate her, and cage her."

She tried to understand Angus' words, but they made no sense as her body writhed in agony.

"Redlynn, you must do it. Find her. Cage her."

Redlynn pushed past the tremors to locate the center of her pain. She inhaled deeply, focusing on her belly. The spot where Adrian had laid his hand the night they lay on the riverbank together. Then she heard it inside. The yowl of a wolf. The being inside her, trying to break free, was her she-wolf. Redlynn saw her in her mind. The she-wolf snarled and snapped, trying to tear free from a small tether that bound her in place. The wolf wanted out. She wanted to run. She wanted Adrian's wolf.

Redlynn tried reasoning with the wolf, tried soothing her. But it didn't work. Another tremor ran through her and her finger bones cracked. She was close to shifting. She was losing control. Her thoughts turned to Adrian, and how she wished he was there with her. At the thought of him, her she-wolf calmed a bit. Redlynn envisioned Adrian's eyes, his face, his body. The touch of his lips to hers, the taste of his breath on her skin. Little by little, the she-wolf backed away. Her cries died down until at last she slumbered, safe and serene.

Redlynn's eye popped open, and she looked down to find her fingers normal. Angus watched her with great intent. When she nodded to him, a broad smile crossed his heavily lined face.

"Well done, lass. Well done." He beamed.

"What was that?" asked Yanti, wide-eyed.

"Redlynn is a she-wolf," said Angus. "The first of our kind."

"A wolf?" The young girl processed the information. A small smile crept over her face. "I wish I was a wolf. Then I'd be a great vampire hunter, like you."

Warmth spread through Redlynn, a self-acceptance she'd never experienced before. For the first time in her life, she knew who she was, and she was proud.

"Let's keep this our little secret for now, okay?" Redlynn said.

"I can keep a secret." Yanti took her hand.

Angus helped Redlynn to her feet, and the three caught up to the girls, several yards ahead. There was a buzz of nervous energy surrounding the group as they walked.

"Red," called Lizzy. "What do we say to our parents?"

"We tell them that you were taken by vampires. That you were saved by wolves, and that you will fight them no more."

"But we've always fought them," said Sasha.

"No," said Redlynn. "We haven't."

The group reached the forest's edge at nightfall. The lights of the huts in Volkzene village still burned bright. With her eyes opened to how much more there was in Fairelle besides Volkzene, it seemed so insignificant now. From their vantage point, Redlynn saw that a Sister stood guard on each gate. It was an improvement, but now, completely unnecessary.

"It'd be best if I remain here." Angus stopped inside the trees. He stared at the village, as if deep in thought.

"If you don't mind... I mean..." Redlynn swallowed. She didn't want Angus to go so soon. "If you'd stay... with me..."

Angus met her eye, and then glanced at the village. He swallowed. "Alright."

Redlynn blew out a sigh of relief. "Thank you. I'll have to try and sneak you past the guard at the gate, but–"

"I know how to get around them." Angus nodded, heading down toward the side of the wooden city wall.

Redlynn watched him leave, and then turned to the girls. She nudged Lizzy forward with an encouraging smile. "Come on."

Word spread like brush fire from house-to-house that she'd returned with the stolen girls. Families ran into the square, screaming and crying for their daughters. The girls ran into their parents' waiting arms, shedding tears of pain and joy. Redlynn stood off to the side, watching the joyous reunions, knowing that

189

there was no one to welcome her, or to shed tears of joy for her return.

Lillith scanned the reunions, her eyes wide in surprise. She spotted Redlynn and headed over. Leaning against the town hall, a fiery anger rose within Redlynn. All these years, Lillith had been filling them with the lies of Adrian's mother, Irina. Did she know the truth, or did she truly believe the lies she'd spread? Somehow, Redlynn doubted it was the latter.

"I forbade you to leave," Lillith said icily. "You disobeyed a direct order."

"I did." Redlynn lifted her chin, standing her ground.

"It's well and good that you brought home our young Sisters, but tomorrow you shall stand before the council and explain why you should not be cast out."

"I *will* stand tomorrow, but not for that." Redlynn spat on the ground, and Lillith sucked in a shocked breath. Redlynn turned and headed for her home. She didn't look back.

When she opened the door, a fire was already lit in the fireplace. Angus had taken several herb jars down from their shelf and was preparing a pot of tea. Redlynn smiled.

"What? You think I don't know how to make tea?" he questioned.

She shrugged and set down her bag. It was strange, being home. All of the things she'd held on to as hers, and cherished of her mother's, seemed no longer important. The herbs and bottles, tea cups and linens, made Redlynn realize just how out of place she truly had been here in the village.

"Are you hungry?" Angus paced like a caged animal. Guilt swept over Redlynn for having asked him to stay.

"I can catch us something." She picked up her bow.

"No, that's not what I meant, lass. I can more than bring us food. I just wondered if you'd eat it."

Angus was trying. A thought occurred to her. "It's hard being here, in my mother's home, isn't it?"

His gaze drifted around and rested on Redlynn's mother's cloak and satchel that still hung by the front door. "She's everywhere here," he whispered. "I can smell her on everything. You smell like her, but different. Like how she would've been, if she'd been a wolf."

"I'm sorry. I can't imagine what you are going through."

"Give it time." He poked the fire and then poured water into the kettle.

"What do you mean?"

"You and Adrian. Being parted from him will cause an undying ache. You were meant for each other. The way Raeleen and I were meant to be together. Only it'll be worse for you, because you two have a destiny together."

"Who says I want to be parted from him?" Redlynn felt her she-wolf stir within her at the thought of being parted from Adrian.

Angus blinked at her, surprised. "Don't you? Isn't that why you came here? To sort out what you are and what you want, the way your mother did?" Angus hung the teapot by the fire and put the herbs away on the shelf.

"And you think I'll make the same choices she did?"

Angus didn't answer. Pulling out a chair, he sat down in it, his weight making it creak.

Would she make the same decision as her mother? She loved Adrian. She didn't want to squander her years in this village, wasting away like her mother. Dying a little inside each time she saw a happy couple walking hand-in-hand with their children. But being with the girls, and seeing the truth behind the lies, woke her up. She couldn't sit by and do nothing. She owed it to the girls to bring about change from how things had been done. She owed it to her mother, as well. Maybe she could divide her time between the two places. Her days in Volkzene and her nights in Wolvenglen.

Redlynn hung her head in her hands, knowing that in the end, she'd have to choose.

"I'll get us something to eat." Angus moved to the door. "I'll stay the night with you, Red, but I can't stay here."

Redlynn nodded, but stayed mute. *Neither can I.*

CHAPTER NINETEEN

The knock came early the next morning, but Redlynn was already awake. Angus came out of her old bedroom, his face stern.

"I made you some breakfast." She pointed to the fire. "I'll be back soon."

"You want me to come?"

She shook her head.

"I won't put up with them hurting ya."

"You'll know if I need you."

Angus nodded and Redlynn pulled open the door. She was greeted by several council members.

"It's time." The mayor peered past her into the house.

Redlynn glanced over her shoulder at Angus looming in the doorway. She shook her head and he backed up as she closed the door.

Stepping down onto the dirt, the council members moved away from her like she was diseased. Slowly, she walked toward the town hall. Unlike the last morning she'd spent in Volkzene, everyone was out this morning. Already having heard the news of the meeting, no doubt, they all wanted to be in attendance. There hadn't been a casting out for close to twenty-five years. Redlynn walked tall, her focus straight ahead, refusing to meet anyone's eye.

When they reached the middle of town, the group turned right, toward the village hall.

The room was already packed with rows and rows of men, women and girls. All of the girls that she'd returned home the night before sat in the front. Above them on a platform sat Lillith, front and center in the largest of chairs. The council members scooted around her and joined Lillith.

Redlynn walked to the middle of the room and faced her sentencers. When everyone was seated, Lillith began the meeting.

"I have called you all here to witness the council's mediation of the proposed casting out of Redlynn of The Sisterhood."

Murmurs could be heard from all sides. Several of the girls spoke to each other in hushed, urgent tones. She stood firm, awaiting her turn to speak.

"I expressly forbade Red from entering the woods, but she disobeyed me and went anyway. To disregard a direct order from The Head Sister demands the punishment of casting out." Lillith's angry gaze trained on her.

"But she saved the girls," came a call from the back. Murmurs of agreement rippled throughout the townsfolk.

"Yes. Yes, she did. But what if she hadn't? What if she'd angered the Weres further, causing them to come and take it out on the rest of us? Our numbers have been dwindling, you all know it. We cannot afford to lose any more of us. We won't survive if we do."

"The wolves won't hurt anyone," said Redlynn.

"Then I suppose it wasn't a Were who killed Anya, and took Sasha and the others?" Lillith countered.

"It was. But that wolf has been killed. He did what he thought best to save his dying pack."

Lillith laughed. "'Did what he thought was best'? And how do you know that?"

"He told me." Her anger rose.

194

Lillith's eyes widened. "That's not possible. The Weres are beasts—"

"No, they aren't. The werewolves are shape-shifting men. They shift into wolf form by choice. They are not our enemy."

Lillith stared at Redlynn, but did not speak. Whispers from the villagers grew louder around the room.

Redlynn pressed on. "It was not always this way between us. The Sisterhood did not always hunt the wolves. They used to be mates to them."

"Lies!" Lillith yelled suddenly, rising from her chair. "You see? She's been brainwashed, like her mother!"

Redlynn had anticipated this. Trying to box her in and discredit her, the way she had Redlynn's mother. Redlynn opened her mouth to speak again.

"No!" yelled Yanti rising from her seat. Yanti's mother tried to pull her down, but Yanti shook her off and walked to stand next to Redlynn. "The wolves helped us. Yes, we were taken by a few, but the rest saved us from the vampires."

"Vampires?" Mayor Helman squeaked.

"Nonsense." Nervousness crossed Lillith's face. "It is obvious that you are still suffering from your ordeal, child."

"I am no longer a child, and I suffer from nothing." Yanti's voice grew stronger. "Yes, it is true. What happened to me, to all of us, is something we aren't likely to forget. When one has been fed upon by vampires for months on end, it tends to leave an impression."

"It's true." Lizzy stood.

Several of the other girls stood as well, and moved to Redlynn's side in support. Forming a line, the girls stared defiantly up into the faces of the council. She looked at them in turn, and smiled to herself. A chill ran through her. Against all her life had taught her, she dared to hope. These were her sisters. These were the future mates to her wolves. These girls standing with her now, who had suffered so much, would change the future of the Sisterhood, and there was nothing Lillith could do about it.

Lillith opened and closed her mouth several times. "This does not change a thing. The fact of the matter is, Red disobeyed me and–"

"Disobeyed what?" Redlynn asked. "Disobeyed your order that I not venture into the woods? Why did you start forbidding us when you became Head of the Order?"

"Because Sisters have gone missing in the woods. I've been trying to protect our way of life."

"No." Redlynn shook her head. "*No*. Sister's have not gone missing in the Wolvenglen Forest."

"My sister Clara lives in Wolvenglen," Lizzy chimed in. "I saw her."

The buzz from the crowd grew louder, and Lillith had to yell to be heard now.

"The forest is dangerous. The Weres–"

"You knew I'd find the truth," Redlynn countered. "You knew that if I went into the forest, I'd discover what you've hidden from us all these years. And we, like stupid sheep, followed blindly without asking questions."

Redlynn turned from the council to face the villagers and other members of the Sisterhood. "You should all know the truth, so you can decide for yourselves. In the beginning, the Sisterhood were mates to the wolves. A hundred years ago, the king of the wolves betrayed his wife. In return for his betrayal, his wife, Sister Irina, took the Sisters and left, vowing to hunt them from that day forward. But no more. Women who we believed to have gone missing live now in Wolvenglen. They bear young with the wolves and live happily. These girls," Redlynn gestured to the line of girls standing beside her, "were taken by a misguided few, led by the vampires. But those men are gone, and the rest of Wolvenglen is committed to keeping us safe from the vampires. As they have done since the beginning."

"Lies!" Lillith yelled.

"Have you not wondered why we dwindle in numbers?" Redlynn's voice rose with frustration. "Why our birth numbers have gone down? Why our Sister ancestors lived to be over one hundred years old, but now we are lucky if we live beyond fifty? It's because *Sisters* were not meant to marry and bear children to farmers. *Sisters* are meant to be with our rightful mates."

"How dare you!" the mayor objected.

"You see?" said Lillith. "You see the lies she spreads? Cast her out, before she has the wolves tearing all of our girls away."

"Was it not you that said you saw three wolves come and take Sasha?" Redlynn yelled. "Then tell me, Lillith, if three wolves took Sasha, how did they get her out?"

Lillith glanced around, refusing to speak.

"If they are not men, if they are beasts only, how did they snatch her up? With their paws? Did they carry her between their jaws? I'll tell you how. Because it was not three wolves, it was two. Two wolves, and a vampire," Redlynn finished.

The crowd burst into an uproar. Yelling sounded all around the hall, bouncing off the walls, and echoing back on itself. Fear crept onto Lillith's face, and she clutched her red stone necklace.

The council huddled together, speaking quickly. Redlynn watched as everything Adrian's mother had tried to build came crumbling down.

"Quiet," said Mayor Helman. "Quiet!"

The noise died down, and everyone took their seats.

"This is a development that we need to discuss as a council. We will adjourn until this evening. At which time, we'll render our decision."

The council walked quickly from the room, followed by Lillith and the whispering crowd. Other members of the sisterhood joined Redlynn, gathering around her.

"What do we do now?" Yanti asked.

"Prepare."

"For what?" asked Sasha.

"For the future. You may no longer need to fight the wolves, but the vampires are still out there. With the death of the vampire king's son, Garot, war will come to both wolves and humans. The wolves will need us at their sides if we are all to succeed."

"Are you going to stay with us?" asked Lizzy.

Redlynn's heart squeezed. They needed her here, but she needed to be with Adrian. Her she-wolf lifted her head to listen for the answer. Redlynn swallowed a lump in her throat. "Let's see what the council decides first."

The day passed slowly for Redlynn. She kept to her home with Angus, who'd changed his mind and refused to leave until there'd been a decision made about her fate.

"What does it matter what they decide, girl? You already know ya aren't stayin' here."

"Because if I leave now, what will that do for the girls? If I stay, and take the judgment, no matter what it is, there will still be hope for the Sisters to return to Wolvenglen. I cannot run from Lillith, because it only reinforces her power over us."

Angus shook his head. "You're just like your mother. I'll never–"

There was a soft knock, interrupting him. Redlynn crossed to the door and pulled it open. There was no one there, but her step was covered in baskets and baskets. She stared at the sight, confused. Flowers and jams, loaves of bread and sweet rolls. Fruits, dried meats, and other miscellaneous items sat waiting.

Redlynn stared at the baskets, not sure what to say. She swallowed hard and tried to hold in the conflicting emotions. The townspeople had never wanted to help her before.

After several trips, she'd brought everything inside. There were anonymous notes attached to many of the baskets. Notes of gratitude for what she'd done, for rescuing their daughters. Several times, Redlynn choked up, overcome with emotion. Eventually she excused herself to her room.

Sitting down on her bed, she let her fingers run over a parchment thank you letter. Why now? Why did they choose to accept me now? *After all this time, after all these years of protecting their houses, their children, their livelihoods. Why now, do they care?*

All those years, her mother had served them, and her mother before her, but now they were finally willing to listen. Finally ready to believe. What had changed?

"It's you." Angus leaned on her doorjamb.

"What?"

"What you were thinking. Why are they doing this now? That was what you were wondering, weren't you?"

"Yes," she whispered.

"It's because you're the one prophesied to return the sisters to the wolves, and to end the shedding of blood."

"What is that?" she asked confused. "Sage said the same thing."

Angus sat next to her heavily on the bed. "One will be born, with the mark of the wolf, to the Sisterhood of Red. And when she finds her destiny, the bloodshed she will end. Taken to bed by the mate of her soul, a reminder she will be. And then will the females follow her home, the cursed will be set free."

"Where's that from?"

"It was the first of the prophecies, given by the mages, to reunite the lands. After the brothers made their wishes to the djinn and the wars started and the prophecies began. No one knows where they came from. All that is known is that the mages wrote them down."

"And you think that is me?"

"Is it? Only you can know."

Redlynn sat silently. Did she know? She'd done most of what Angus had said. It was possible.

Redlynn smiled as Angus left the room. A pain hit her gut. Her she-wolf awoke again, letting out a mournful whine. Her thoughts turned to Adrian. More than ever she wished she'd asked him to come. Memories of his lips on hers, and his eyes when they'd said goodbye the day before, loomed over her.

"Mother," she whispered. "What do I do now?"

CHAPTER TWENTY

Adrian ran through the woods; a giant white bear followed behind. His anger toward his mother had raged over the past week. The first night after Redlynn had left, he thought he might actually die. The pain of knowing that she wasn't near was almost too much for him to handle.

By the second night, he'd taken to the bottle to dull the pain, and Dax had taken to checking on him every couple of hours. When Angus didn't return on the third day, Adrian had resigned himself to the fact that she'd decided to stay in Volkzene, Angus as well. He couldn't blame Angus. Angus had lost his mate. To lose his daughter so soon after finding her would be all that much harder.

Adrian sprinted across the riverbank where he'd held her in his arms, and his heart ached all the more. He'd done what he was supposed to. He'd taken the throne and seized command of the wolves. But without Redlynn, it was all for naught. He was as powerless as he'd been before he'd met her.

He'd started coming out to the woods to run the last two nights. Dax, the white bear, had joined him, probably afraid he might do something stupid, like run into Tanah Darah. Last night, Adrian had found himself at the edge of the woods, overlooking the village of Volkzene for hours on end. The villagers were busy celebrating the return of their daughters. From his vantage point, he'd tried to catch a glimpse of Redlynn, but hadn't seen her. Tonight, he'd resigned himself to the fact that she wasn't coming back, and he hadn't returned to Volkzene. Instead, he'd run in the opposite direction.

Running with no other purpose but to make himself forget, Adrian sprinted over rocks and fallen tree limbs. He cleared the river in an enormous bound and continued on, down into the valley.

Dax didn't pry. He didn't speak; he was good like that. He simply followed along, making sure Adrian was safe. The giant bear's company was so different than Blain's had been. Blain had been chatty and witty, but Dax was reserved. A quiet strength that Adrian appreciated having at his back. But his camaraderie with Dax wouldn't last much longer. He'd seen a restlessness in Dax. He'd move on soon. Most likely to finally face his demons and figure out who he was.

Adrian darted past the rocks where they'd found Lizzy, and out into the clearing where Redlynn had howled at the moon. He stopped in the middle, panting hard. The stars twinkled like candle flames, flickering far away. Breathing deep, he took in the scents around him. He sat on his haunches, remembering the last time he'd seen her, the wolf, in the woods. The way she'd looked so happy howling at the moon.

A rustle in the trees caught his attention, and Adrian turned around. Silence. Sniffing, he caught no scent. All sounds ceased except for the chirp of an occasional locust.

"Dax?" Adrian called.

There was no answer.

"Dax?" he called again. A shiver ran down his spine.

"I'm heading to the castle. You take your time," Dax said.

Adrian listened as something moved closer. He flattened his belly to the ground, trying to hide himself amongst the tall grass. He scanned the opposite end of the clearing. A form emerged from the darkness. A large red wolf with golden eyes made her way into the moonlight. He hopped up, his heart beating wildly.

"Hello."

Adrian's breath caught. She'd come back. She'd really come back.

"Hello," Adrian whispered.

"May I come in?"

Adrian stared in disbelief.

Redlynn shifted from foot to foot. *"Maybe I should just–"*

"Don't go," he said, quickly regaining his composure. He took a step closer to her and she took a step closer as well.

"You came back," he said softly.

"I told you I would."

"I know, but–"

"If you don't want me here, I'll leave."

How could she say that? How could she think he wouldn't want her? *"Why would I want you to leave?"*

She didn't answer. The two circled each other slowly, each taking in the sight and smells of the other.

"You learned how to shift."

"Angus has been teaching me."

It all seemed so unreal. Just when he'd resigned himself to losing her forever, she was here, in the woods, in wolf form.

"Are the girls alright?" he asked.

"The girls are fine. I was made Head of the Order."

Adrian's throat went dry and his heart sank. She wasn't staying.

"Lillith knew, not only about the wolves, but about the vampires as well. She said nothing about the vampires, because it would've exposed the lies she'd told about the wolves. But I think it went deeper than that."

"What did you do with her?"

203

"Nothing. When the Council went to pronounce her sentence of banishment, she was gone."

"Gone?"

"Only a few things were found missing. Enough to fill a pack, no more."

"Where did she go?"

"No one knows. But I have a feeling we'll see her again. I don't think she alone worked on keeping the Sisters from the Wolves."

"That's good," he finally said, sitting down. "I mean about you being made Head of the Order, not about Lillith. They need you."

"Yes, I suppose they do."

"Did Angus teach you how to communicate in wolf form as well?"

"He did." She cocked her head to the side. "How old are you?"

"What?"

"Angus told me that wolves live longer than humans. So it got me wondering how old you are."

"Old."

"And me? How long will I live?"

He hoped it was for as long as he did. "I don't know."

Redlynn let out a heavy breath. The air around her vibrated and she whimpered. Adrian watched as her body contorted and flexed, her limbs retracting, red fur giving way to smooth skin. A cry escaped her and he wanted to run to her.

After she finished and she lay panting on the ground, gaining her bearings, he too shifted. When he looked up, she stood naked in the moonlight. His heart caught in his throat as desire wracked him. Her hair hung loosely, covering her breasts and womanhood. Her long, slender legs were creamy and smooth. He couldn't stand, for fear she'd see his arousal.

204

"Adrian," she finally said. "I don't want to play games anymore. If I've learned one thing in these last weeks, it's that I need to speak my mind. I know you're hurting because of Blain. You're questioning your own existence because of what he did. You're also afraid. Afraid of being hurt. I understand that."

She took a step closer to him.

"But I also know that I am the one. The one from the prophecy, but most of all, I know that I'm the one for you. I'm yours. I love you in a way that I honestly never thought possible. And I want to be with you. Now and forever. If you need time to–"

She didn't get a chance to finish her sentence. Adrian crossed to her. His lips on hers, he pulled her close, smashing her body into his. *She loves me.*

*****

Redlynn's body tremored with anxiety. Spilling her feelings to Adrian made her more nervous than when she'd faced the village council. But if they were ever going to make this work, one of them was going to have to start the conversation. Bags shadowed his eyes and he was unshaven. All she wanted to do was rush to him, but he sat there, listening to her ramble.

Then, before she knew what was happening, he was on her. His lips on hers, his strong arms wrapping her in to him. It made her head spin at the smell of him. She'd missed him so much. He lifted her off the ground, kissing her with fervor. His tongue plunged into her mouth, twisting and dancing with hers. His warm lips crushed hers with his power. A moan escaped her as his lips travelled down her chin to her neck. He nipped and licked her skin.

"I love you. I love you. I love you," he said over and over as he kissed her.

She dug her nails into his shoulders and he set her down on the grass, running his hands over her body.

Redlynn gasped for air. Tingling skittered over her skin, setting her ablaze. She shuddered at his touch and found herself unwittingly moving her hands over the muscles of his broad chest to his back, and lower. They allowed their hands an opportunity to explore each other.

His hands roamed and caressed her flesh until she thought she might burst. The heat that pooled inside of her burned hotter the longer they kissed. The scent he gave off told her everything she needed to know. He marked her, making it known to all other males, that she was his. Just as she was marking him with her own scent.

"Adrian," she whispered as he kissed her shoulder. "You're killing me."

He chuckled softly. "Is this not what you want, my love?"

"No," she said roughly. "And it's not what you want either." Planting her hands firmly on his chest, she flipped him over. The fire sparkling in his eyes told Redlynn she was right. Soft and gentle was not how they wanted it. She straddled his hips with hers, but didn't allow their bodies to merge.

"What beautiful eyes you have," she murmured.

"The better to see you with, my love."

She reached up and traced his lips with her finger. "What beautiful lips you have," she whispered.

"The better to kiss you with, my love."

Redlynn bent down and kissed him hard on the mouth. Adrian groaned and thrust his hips toward hers, but she pulled away.

"What a glorious body you have," she said.

"The better to love you with, my queen," he whispered in her ear.

Wasting no more time, Redlynn licked his chest, taking his salty taste in her mouth.

"Redlynn." The veins in his neck strained and corded. "I need you."

His fingers dug into her hips and at that moment, they became mates. The feeling of joining with him exploded inside her in painful ecstasy. A tear escaped her eye. This was who she was and what she was meant for. She dug her nails into his shoulders and bent over, kissing him hard. Their rhythm increased, warmth pooling inside her belly and spreading out from there. Tingling spread from her thighs up her back. Every fiber of her body was on fire. Moments later, Adrian's roar was only second to the one that Redlynn released.

It was complete. She was Redlynn, Queen of the Weres.

EPILOGUE

Redlynn pulled a brush through Baleen's tangled hair.

"Hold still, wiggly." She laughed.

"Can't help it, mama, I'm so excited."

"Well, we'll never get out of here, if you don't let your mother finish," said Adrian, playing with their son, Fergus, on the bed. Redlynn turned toward him and Adrian winked at her.

"Yes, Dada." Baleen turned her golden eyes on him.

Adrian picked up a rattle from the bed and shook it at Fergus.

"Ball!" Fergus giggled.

"Rattle," said Adrian.

"Ball."

Redlynn smiled and tied Baleen's long, red hair up with a ribbon. "There. Done."

"Yeah, yeah, yeah! We go now?"

"Yes," said Adrian. "We go now."

"Yippie!" Baleen screeched, jumping from her stool and running out into the hall. "Papa Angus! Papa Angus! We leave now," she cried, running down to the dining hall.

Adrian laughed, stood from the bed, and handed Fergus to Yanti.

"Will you tell my parents hello for me?" Yanti settled Fergus on her hip.

"Of course." Redlynn smiled.

"Travel safe." Yanti took Fergus, cooed at him, and walked to his room next door.

Yanti had joined them in Wolvenglen just that year. She was too young to mate. But the sixteen-year-old, blond-haired beauty had many suitors among the pack. It wouldn't be long before Adrian performed the bonding ritual on Yanti and her chosen mate.

Redlynn stood slowly from her seat, supporting her lower back. Adrian was at her side in an instant.

"Maybe we should wait this year." He laid his palm on Redlynn's extended belly.

"Hanna checked me over. I'm not due for another three months. She said I would be fine to make the trip. I just can't shift."

Adrian's face held concern. She pressed her own palm on top of his as he stroked her womb. Redlynn's she-wolf slapped her tail in satisfaction.

"It will be okay." The child inside kicked and moved at his touch. Adrian smiled and bent, kissing her stomach. She sighed and stroked his soft hair. He looked up at her, his concern still apparent. "I'll be fine, my love. Besides, you know I have to go at least twice a year. Once for Initiations, once for Settlings."

Adrian shook his head. "It's not that. It's been years since we rescued the girls. The vampires have been silent for far too long. We've not seen anything of them since finding Lillith's mangled body at the northern border, next to their lands."

"I know." She laid her hand on his stubbly cheek.

"Even Sage has seen nothing in his travels. They're quiet. Too quiet."

"Perhaps it is because of what Sage said. They know that their prophecy is next. Perhaps they're scared."

"Or building their ranks." Adrian stood and wrapped his arms around her waist. "War is coming, and I don't want you and our young caught in the middle."

"Which is why we need as many Sisters as possible. Today is a good day. Five new Sisters will be mated to their chosen, Adrian. Remember what that felt like for us? The day I met you in the woods and we became one? Today that happens for Paulo, Law, Athos, Marcos and Rue. More Sisters, more mates, more young."

Adrian nodded and pulled her close. "I only care about one Sister."

She took in his heavenly scent, something she never grew tired of. She hadn't regretted returning to him for even a moment. In the years since she'd returned the girls to Volkzene, she still wasn't used to being Head of the Order. However, knowing that she wouldn't be staying in the village permanently, she'd set up both a second and a third in her stead. And several of the wolves had taken up the position of emissaries with the Sisterhood, bringing messages back and forth.

Wrapping her arms around Adrian's broad chest, she laid her cheek on his shoulder. His hands rubbed down her spine to her rump. He lowered his lips to her neck, and she felt a familiar tingle in her thighs.

"Adrian," she moaned.

"Yes, my mate?"

"We have somewhere to be."

"I know." He slid her gown off her shoulder, kissing her bare skin while running his finger over her bodice.

"Adrian," she growled.

"Yes, my lover?"

"Just once."

"Of course, my queen."

Fairelle Book Two

By Rebekah R. Ganiere

The Border of Wolvenglen Forest and The Daemonlands, Fairelle
Year 1210 A.D. (After Daemons)
CHAPTER ONE

Sage sprinted through the dark after his prey, his vampiric sight guiding his every move. The would-be assassins rushed away from him, registering as light blue blurs in the night. Their vampiric heat signatures registering as cool as his own.

A hulking ivory bear thundered behind him.

"Keep up, Dax!" he yelled over his shoulder.

Dax bounded over a fallen tree trunk and growled a reply.

A branch whipped Sage in the face, opening a cut below his right eye. *Dammit that stings.*

He tracked the vampires over a rock less than thirty yards ahead of him before they disappeared from view. Picking up speed, he headed for it.

He rounded a tree, came to the rock and halted. An assassin waited for him several yards away. Sage recognized him as one of his own former guards.

"Your uncle, King Philos, sends his regards, usurper," the vampire yelled, lobbing something directly at him.

Sage spun to the left, but the object caught his side, slicing him open. The white knife, with a blood red-handle lodged in a tree behind him. Sage hissed. *A ceremonial Cris.*

Dark blood oozed through his fingers and hit the ground in fat drops. Rounding on the vampire he bared his fangs, but the vampire was gone. Poison blasted through him like brushfire.

Sage yanked the Cris from the tree and shoved it in his waistband. Philos would be angered by the loss of yet another Cris knife. He couldn't have more than a couple left. Too bad for him, it was Sage's now.

Dax caught up and slowed to a halt before sniffing him.

"I'll be fine." Sage scanned the area for his prey once more.

A whistling sound grew louder. Sage planted his hands in Dax's thick fur and shoved him out of the way with tremendous effort. An arrow flew through the trees where they'd just stood, and continued past them into the darkness.

"Tell Adrian they're by the northern border. If he cares to catch up, we could use some help."

Dax snorted and nodded.

Sage took off again at a slower pace. The mental connection between the Weres had come in quite handy since he'd taken to helping them patrol the borders of Wolvenglen Forest for the intruding vampires from the north. Those in Tanah Darah were loyal to his uncle, which meant they had no qualms about heading into human cities to find food. In return, Sage had no qualms about killing them.

His wound continued to seep through his fingers; his vampiric healing ability was of no use against a Cris. He hadn't told Dax the total truth. Yes, he would be fine – if he got to his den in the next two hours. If he didn't, the poison would attack his heart and he would bleed out. And if that happened…well…he'd need something stronger than squirrel blood to help him out of that situation.

Dax moved silently beside him. Sounds of a battle drifted from up ahead.

As Sage maneuvered through the trees, his pain intensified. Tendrils of daemon magick from the gash in his side curled their way through his body. He grimaced and braced himself on the nearest tree trunk. The burning sensation threaded up over his ribs and across the small of his back causing the muscles to tighten and cramp. Taking in a long, low breath, he tried to stave off what he knew was coming.

A series of howls rang out behind him. He glanced over his shoulder. King Adrian, Queen Redlynn, Angus, and several other wolves appear out of the tree line.

The group advanced to the edge of an outcropping at the northern border of the forest. Adrian and Dax shifted into human form next to Sage and peered down at the clearing below.

Sage's gaze moved to the dark hills of his homeland that lay beyond the valley. His gut clenched at the sight. *Tanah Darah.* The dark craggy terrain jutted straight up, surrounding the vampire lands in a giant wall. Only a narrow path connected Tanah Darah to the rest of Fairelle.

"Who's down there?" asked Adrian

Sage glanced at the naked Were King. His tall strong body was covered in sweat and clumps of shaggy dark hair clung to his neck and shoulders.

"Vampire assassins again, sent by my uncle. I'm not sure who the newcomers are," Sage said.

A dozen figures fought in the grassy basin between Tanah Darah and Wolvenglen. The remaining five vampires he and Dax had been chasing viciously attacked seven men dressed in black. He squinted and focused on the battle. His vampiric night-vision registered the vampires as light-blue, pale forms, the ones they fought glowed with a golden essence. He'd never seen anything like it.

3

The golden-hued newcomers took the upper hand. They fought with skill and grace pushing the vampires toward Wolvenglen and away from their escape path.

He studied the golden figures in an effort to discern who they were. Fae possibly, or– A shiver ran through him. *It can't be.*

"The black-clad figures must have ambushed the vampires." Dax scratched his broad, hairless chest with hands almost the same size of his bear paws and then brushed his blond locks from his eyes. "They had to be waiting. But who are they? And why?"

The vampires were quick by nature, but the golden-hued figures were equal in skill. The tallest among them produced a white-bladed Cris knife, and cleanly sliced the head off a vampire. The vampire fell to his knees and collapsed.

Sage swallowed hard. *One of the golden figures has a Cris knife.* A jolt of pain raced through him and he took a deep breath. He lifted his gaze to the sky. There were still several hours left before the sun came up, but he would need healing before then.

The fighting continued below. From their vantage point, the group watched the black-clad figure work together to take down their foes. Unlike the vampires who fought only for themselves.

After the last vampire fell, the strangers took a moment to regroup.

"We should go," said Dax. "We don't know who they are."

"No." Adrian shook his head. "If they fight the vampires, then we should speak with them. We could use more allies."

One of the men below looked up in Sage's direction. He grabbed an arrow from his quiver, notched it and shot, alerting his comrades. The others in his group followed suit. Adrian, Dax and the wolves moved out of the line of fire, into the trees, but Sage remained, transfixed. He swatted an arrow away from his face and caught another before it pierced his chest.

After the volley of missed shots, the figures hustled silently up the hillside. They fanned out to the quickest and easiest routes, moving with the ease and precision of a team that had fought together for years. They just couldn't be. But they were too good. There was no other explanation.

A feeling of dread ran down Sage's spine and skittered over his skin. His muscles spasmed in pain again and his knees almost buckled. The Cris poison coursed its way through him.

A breeze lifted the men's scents to him and he breathed them in. Their blood carried an aroma he'd not encountered before. His mouth pooled with saliva and for the first time in years, he craved the taste of human blood. Need pulsed through him as his fangs ached to bite into something. *This was bad.*

Adrian joined him once more. "Dax is right. We should go. This is obviously not the time for talking."

A figure crouched behind a shrub and shot another arrow. The arrow landed at Redlynn's feet and she yelped in surprise. Adrian howled in rage and charged toward the edge of the cliff. His skin rippled, ready to shift.

Sage caught him by the shoulder. "No, King Adrian," he said. "They're humans. They're just doing their job. They aren't after you or Redlynn, they're after me."

Adrian's gaze met Sage's. His eyes turned golden and fur burst from his skin, under Sage's hand. "Why do they want you?"

Sage was barely able to choke the words out. "They're Vampire Slayers."

Thank you for taking the time to read
Red the Were Hunter

If you enjoyed the book, please take a moment to leave a review on
your favorite retailer.

Look for the next books in the series:
Snow the Vampire Slayer (Book Two)
Jamen's Yuletide Bride (Book Two and a Half)
Zelle and the Tower (Book Three)
&
Cinder the Fae (Book Four)

Yanti's Choice – Free Fairelle Short Story

To find out more about **Rebekah R. Ganiere** and *The Fairelle Series*, or her other Upcoming Releases, or to join her Newsletter for Swag and Freebies, Please connect with her in the following places:

BOOKS WITH A BITE
Newsletter: www.RebekahGaniere.com/Newsletter
Goodreads: www.Goodreads.com/VampWereZombie
Twitter: www.Twitter.com/VampWereZombie
Facebook: www.Facebook.com/VampiresWerewolvesZombies

Award Winning–Bestselling Author
Rebekah R. Ganiere

<u>Fairelle Series</u>
Red the Were Hunter (Book One)
Snow the Vampire Slayer (Book Two)
Jamen's Yuletide Bride (Book Two & a Half)
Zelle and the Tower (Book Three)
Cinder the Fae (Book Four)
Belle and the Beast (Fall 2016)
Yanti's Choice – Free Fairelle Short Story

<u>The Otherworlder Series</u>
Saving Christmas
Cupid's Curse
Haunting Halloween (Oct. 2016)

<u>The Society Series</u>
Reign of the Vampires
Rise of the Fae
Vengeance of the Demons

<u>Shifter Rising Series</u>
Promised at the Moon
Cursed by the Moon

Shifter Rising Spin off Series
<u>Wolf River</u>
Reclaiming His Mate

Dead Awakenings
Kissed by the Reaper

www.RebekahGaniere.com